Scheherazade

AND THE AMBER NECKLACE

*

GORDON
THOMPSON

CLOUDS OF MAGELLAN PRESS

ISBN: (Paperback) 978-0-6451935-0-3
ISBN: (ebook) 978-0-6451935-4-1

Published by Clouds of Magellan Press, Melbourne
http://cloudsofmagellanpress.net

Cover: Lucinda Gifford
http://lucindagiffordbooks.com

Publication and distribution, Lightning Source, through eBook Alchemy.
http://ebookalchemy.com.au

for Lara, Maya, Daniel, and Genevieve

CONTENTS

prologue ... 1

Part 1 – The Apricot Tree ... 5

Part 2 – The Journey ... 45

Part 3 – Ishaq and the Flying Carpet ... 101

Part 4 – The Beast King ... 139

Part 5 – The Battle ... 181

Acknowledgements

Scheherazade

AND THE AMBER NECKLACE

Prologue

'Is the moon coming home with us?' said Scheherazade with a yawn.

It was the Night of Nights. Scheherazade was seven years old. Her father, Jafar, was carrying her in his arms. Between the trees, the yellow moon seemed to be following her, drifting along the sky.

'No,' said Jafar, stroking her hair. 'And are you not asleep? The Moon *wants* to come with us, and she will even peek in at the window later, but she must stay where she is, up there in the heavens.'

'Why? She could sleep in our room. I could put a rug on the floor.'

She heard her mother, Marjanah, give a little laugh. In her arms, Marjanah held the sleeping Dunyazad.

'I think there would be room,' said Jafar, 'but, once, not so long ago, when the world was young, the Moon was walking by the sea, and there she heard singing. It turned out to be the voice of a handsome young fisherman, named Mesh ibn Utu, and he was mending his nets in the blue midnight. Now, though it was forbidden for a goddess to seek the joys of mortals, she fell in love with the young fisherman and took him to her beautiful house in the deep, deep, deep of the sea. And there ...'

Marjanah gave a little cough.

'There, they lost track of time. But then Isimud, the messenger of the gods, discovered them together. Oosh!

Unhappy day. The gods were angry and threw a heavenly stone that struck the young fisherman – right here on the side of the head – and killed him. And the Moon … well, after that, she was forced to stay in the realm of the gods and behave like an immortal. No longer allowed to walk the forests, only permitted to look at this world from afar. And on a night such as this, do you see? She is looking, and remembering Mesh ibn Utu. And when she remembers she weeps tears that fall into the Great River.'

Scheherazade could see the glittering yellow tears flashing on the surface of the river. She yawned.

'But all is not lost. Those tears turn into beautiful pieces of amber,' said Jafar, 'which is a magic jewel that lets you see into the future. So … there it is. The End. Goodnight.'

'I'm going to gather up all the amber,' said Dunyazad, Scheherazade's younger sister, who had woken up to listen.

'Tomorrow we can look,' said Jafar.

'Amber is special,' said Dunyazad.

'It is,' said Jafar. 'Special and rare.'

'If you rub it you can look in it and see who you will marry …'

'Yes,' said Jafar. 'So I have heard.'

'I'm going to make a necklace of amber and see all the men I might marry.'

Scheherazade rolled her eyes.

'Time to sleep,' said Marjanah.

'That reminds me of a story about an amber necklace,' said Jafar as they walked on. 'A young prince once found a necklace of amber that could …'

'Enough,' said his wife, putting on the low voice that she used for chiding the dog. 'They will never sleep if you keep babbling …'

'Babbling? You call this babbling!?' said Jafar. 'I'll have you know I won third prize in the Festival of Storytellers in Samarkand.'

'Ah, now there's a story,' said Marjanah. 'Tell *that* to the girls, that'll put us all to sleep.'

'You've asked for it now,' said Jafar. 'Once upon a time, not so long ago, there was a famous storyteller. He was a strikingly handsome fellow, who went one day to Samarkand …'

They walked on through the forest under the watching moon.

Part 1

The Apricot Tree

*

ରେ After Tarquin deposed his father Montague, and
became king of Edessa, he quickly proved himself to be a
warlike and dangerous fool. But one day, reports of a
disturbing nature came to the court. It was said that the
king of the neighbouring land, Zayn Al-Asnam, had
sent agents to search for, and they had found, a magic
carpet in a cave in the Zagros Mountains. This carpet, it
was said, could carry a stealthy assassin into the most
protected room of the most fortified citadel. Tarquin
sent delegates to Al-Asnam and demanded that he
confirm or deny the rumours. Al-Asnam laughed in the
face of the emissaries, his folded hands bouncing up and
down on his stomach. But Tarquin became convinced
that a mysterious assassin riding on a carpet with purple
tassels would infiltrate the palace, and it would be the
end of him.

from The Nights of Abu Nuwas

1

The Days of Happiness

Jafar had once worked as a scribe under the old king Montague. Starting as a simple copyist he progressed to the position of 'Distinguished Writer of Letters'. Sitting next to the generals and the ministers in their counsels, he helped them give voice to their policies. It was a fortunate time. Jafar had his own little room in the palace and would return home at the end of every second day. Sipping his mint tea he would ask his wife about the day, about the girls' schooling, then say, 'Today I wrote a long letter of praise to the Chief Minister of Belugo and noted his shrewdness, his percipience, his acuity, his abundant perspicacity! I found thirty-three different words to honour his wisdom.'

'Only thirty-three?' said Marjanah. 'You must have had a bad morning. And is this man truly perspicacious?'

'I never met him,' said Jafar, raising his glass of tea.

On the evenings when he was not working at the palace, Jafar went with his family a short walk to the next village. Their destination was Ajedro's Bookshop and Antiquary, where a crowd gathered in the evening to listen to stories. Jafar was always welcome, for he was a skilled storyteller. Scheherazade loved to watch as people drew close, leaning in to hear the magic of her father's voice. He would recite Mardukka and his Magic Jackdaw, or the Tale of Ali Baba and the Forty Thieves,

Sinbad the Sailor. Sometimes it seemed that the stars leant in to listen.

Ajedro was a good friend to the family. He had come from northern lands, across the Middle Sea, with several boxes full of books and curios. He had prospered in the village. As well as the books and antiques, he sold coffee and what he called *pastillos*. Ajedro had straggly hair that flew out from under his cap, and a pet monkey named Tonto that wore a red beret and an embroidered jacket. The monkey, who was extremely shy, could be persuaded to put the smaller books and items back on the shelves in return for pistachios. Tonto made very little noise for a monkey, just a sniffing that sounded to Scheherazade as if he was holding back tears.

Jafar bought books and small ornaments at the shop. Ajedro also enjoyed giving little gifts to the girls. Then there would be talk outside under the lanterns, and then the storytelling.

Jafar, however, was not as good a storyteller as Massoud Al Jazir. Massoud had won *first* prize in Samarkand several times running and was one of two storytellers employed by the palace. And he made a point of always wearing his prize scarf with its little gold medallions.

This bothered Jafar, who had only come third in Samarkand. 'Perhaps it is that he has a deeper voice than I have. It's the heavy chin that does it. He is a fine storyteller, yes, but really ... Number One? Samarkand's finest?'

'There is no justice,' said Marjanah with a tolerant smile.

'You're right, there is no justice.'

Jafar hated it whenever Massoud came to the storytelling outside Ajedro's shop, but he put on a brave face and clapped the loudest when Massoud finished speaking. And kept his annoyance hidden when Massoud's daughter, Amirah, was invited to sing or to speak. The girl had talent, for sure. But Jafar was quietly confident that Dunyazad, his younger daughter, would fulfil his dreams of fame by surpassing Amirah.

Dunyazad had a sweet tongue and had inherited her father's gift with words.

However, Scheherazade could not tell a story to save her life. She could sing, and prattle nonsense to a little child when required; but when asked by her father to tell a story in the grand style (or any style) the words stuck in her throat like a dry date. He no longer bothered to ask.

So, Jafar put his hope in Dunyazad, that hers would be the name that people spoke; or else that Massoud might fall off his mule and crack his head open, thus leaving Jafar free to make a final run for Samarkand, and the little statue of Seneca, and a prize scarf decorated with gold medallions.

But fate has a strange way of healing imagined hurts. Marjanah died one night of a sudden fever, and Jafar had to wake the girls to tell them what had happened. The day stole upon them, empty and cold. Massoud had hurried to the house and seemed as stricken as any of their friends. 'Whatever you need, Jafar, anything. Just name it,' he said. And Massoud and his wife brought meals every second day for three months as the family grieved. Jafar was grateful to him for ever after.

Life resumed – it had a way of bustling about, and scratching on the door early in the morning. Soon the family went back to listening to stories at Ajedro's shop; but Scheherazade, often as not, just sat there, toying with the sack of emptiness she'd been handed.

One day, when the girls had grown, Jafar found himself out of favour at the palace. He came home in the early afternoon. His daughters found him at home when they returned from school.

'Father, what has happened?' asked Scheherazade.

'Today,' said Jafar massaging his brow with his fingertips, 'I wrote that the Prince of Astragonne was in the precarious position of a newly hatched duckling that has strayed too far from its mother, and is too foolish to see that it plays near the whiskers of the sleeping fox; or again, like the chittering monkey that runs along a branch that hangs low over the glittering river, without the wit to see the waiting crocodile that knows the meaning of patience … It was a sweet, elegant letter. But the king struck it all out and had Ali Besan write instead, "Pay up, or die". So, the king will be busy tomorrow and the next day and the next and pity the Prince of Astragonne and the poor people who fall under his care. And since actions speak louder than words, all the scribes have been given the next few months off, without pay!'

'Will we starve, Papa?' said Dunyazad.

'My sister will give us bread. And she has said that you can come to work for her. We have our little vegetable garden, and the fruit trees …' His voice went river-like, as if he had arrived at a very important part of the story. 'You know, that if anything went dreadfully wrong, you should go to Ajedro? If I am not here, he will be as a father to you. I … I have spoken with him.'

The girls did not understand, but they ran and embraced Jafar. After this they both began to work in their Aunt Paribanou's bakery, and Jafar sat at home sharpening his quills, waiting to be summoned to the palace. He began to look like a robe hung out to dry.

2

The King Goes Hunting

The king of Edessa was Tarquin the Conqueror. Tall, fair-skinned, golden-haired. To many, he was known as Tarquin the Dangerous. He won his first battle at age sixteen, had taken his first minor kingdom at seventeen, and was king of the realm at age twenty after his father, Montague, fled into exile, in fear of his ambitious son. Tarquin worried a lot about the thinness of his beard. His exiled father, who had been known as Montague the Peacemaker, had come with *his* father, Henry the Destroyer, from the northern lands of Archenistan in the Days of Destruction. The armies had been called the white angels of death. Henry had made a pact with Akkadia, the vast empire to the south, and what had been the small emirate of Al'moheda was no more.

A new palace was built on the eastern side of the Great River, on the ruins of the old city. Beyond, where the sun rose, the land was desert and the ruins of older kingdoms lay scattered there. Sometimes, on hot days, a great head with a broken crown could be seen through the rippling currents of air.

In front of the palace, a bridge spanned the river, joining the older lands of advancing desert to the fresher forests of the western hills.

The river and its connections had, over time, made Al'moheda a place of trade. But under Tarquin, Edessa now had a new industry. When not playing polo, or raising monuments in praise of himself, Tarquin made war. He made it as easily as a hen lays an egg, and in the same random way – you never quite knew where they would turn up. The inlaid marble and gold walls of the New Palace had caused a famine, but Tarquin remedied this by sacking the grain silos of the Grassland Kingdoms in a lightning attack.

But the king was also a reader and loved stories. His favourite books were tales of the Greek heroes, tales of men who had become gods, and books of military victories. His wife, Queen Amytis, was also learned. After extravagant dinners when the guests had all stumbled away, or been carried off, the queen would enchant the king with tales of her land (for she was a daughter of the Sultan of Akkadia). And the moon shone upon the Great River, and Amytis would sing. It was one of the few times when the king did not move restlessly. At all other times his foot bounced constantly, as if he was, even at rest, spurring on a horse, or getting ready to sprint into battle.

Tarquin's other favourite pastime was hunting. No-one knew when the king would ride into the forest. But when that happened, the villagers knew to keep well back from the horses and hounds.

One day, Scheherazade heard a rumbling, like trees falling. The dull sound gathered strength and from it spilled the jangle of harness bells and drumming hooves, and the goosey honk of hunting horns. The sound came closer. They heard old Mozir hurrying to find his goats, calling out, gathering them in. It was the Day of Silence, when a gentle quiet would pervade the village after the songs and chanting in the temple of Nabu. But that silence was now finished.

Dunyazad seemed excited by the clamour.

'Do you think it is the king?! Come!' she said.

'No! Where are you going?' said Scheherazade.

But Dunyazad was already out of the house and in the yard. Scheherazade followed.

'O, I'm scared!' said Dunyazad. 'What if we see him?' She grabbed Scheherazade's hand and dragged her to the cluster of apricot trees that ranged along the back of their yard. She began to climb. 'I want to see him. Come on. They will ride past. We can look.'

'Are you mad? Don't!'

'No-one will see us,' said Dunyazad. She already had a sandalled foot on the lower branch. Because their father was still at the temple, and because Scheherazade was a little bit older than Dunyazad, she climbed as well, hissing, 'Take care. D! Don't spoil the fruit!'

The two largest of the apricot trees leaned out over the wall and over the path that ran behind their home. Dunyazad was clambering up the first tree, but Scheherazade chose the other, for all the branches were laden with fruit and two bodies on one branch would have been too much for the wood to bear. Scheherazade hid herself in the dark green leaves and looked across at her sister. Dunyazad's face had the same look she wore when she was lost in a story. Dunyazad was now as high up and as far out on the branch as was wise, and then a little bit more.

Twelve black and muscled horses raced down the forest path and up to the wall. Scheherazade felt the breeze of them on her face and could smell the horses. The rumble caused fruit to fall – or else it was her trembling that shook the branch.

More horses raced up and she shrank further into the leaves. One horse had stopped. She heard directly beneath her the *clingk-cling* of spurs, the hissing of breath – horse and man. Scheherazade pulled herself tight against the branch and closed her eyes. But a close noise made her open them again. A gloved hand, like a small pheasant hopping along the branch, appeared, searched around, plucked an apricot, and vanished.

She heard a sound of lips smacking and a voice declaring, 'This is perfection.'

She looked down. It was the king. She recognised him from the face on the coins. Usually one only saw the white-skinned foreigners from a distance. But the king was close enough that if Scheherazade had picked an apricot and thrown it, she could have hit him on the nose.

Scheherazade tried to stop breathing. The king's eyes did not see her (or did not acknowledge seeing her) in her green and orange sari that blended so well with the leaves and fruit. But he was alert to something nearby. He moved to the next tree.

Was it really the king? It was the other voices that confirmed it – hearty and deferential. 'What have you found, o my Lord?' 'What new prize is this, my Lord?' 'The fruit is easier to reach here, my Lord'.

There was a pause.

'It most certainly is!' said the king.

Scheherazade knew something was happening, because she heard a horse shaking its harness bells and the sound seemed strange and loud. And all the other conversations had stopped. She could see nothing.

'And what fruit is this?' said the king.

Dunyazad answered him.

> *It is the apricot, known as the precocious one,*
> *It shines in a sweet brightness of golden velvet.*
> *It makes heavy the green branch,*
> *It is the saffron moon,*
> *Injured easily by untimely frost or strong wind.*

Scheherazade had to admire the answer. She couldn't put words together like that.

'Your words are as sweet as the fruit of these trees,' said the king. 'Is this your father's house?'

'It is, my Lord.'

'And what did you just recite?

'It is from the Secret Night of Ibn Al-Muqqafa.'

'And what's your name, who perches in a tree offering fruit, with sweet verses upon her lips?'

'I am Dunyazad, the daughter of Jafar and Marjanah, may she rest in peace.'

'Jafar – one of the scribes,' said a voice.

'Former scribe,' said another.

'Pass me another one of the apricots,' said the king.

Scheherazade listened to the rustling of leaves and the little *stp* sound of the stalk snapping. Another sound, a laugh, more a breath exhaled through nostrils.

Scheherazade leant a little to one side and saw two hands glancing against each other, as if pulling away.

Cries and yelps and blaring horns suddenly broke from a thicket a little way off. 'It comes near!' called a man.

'Be careful that you do not fall, daughter of Jafar,' said the king. He cried out, 'Yaah!' and spurred his horse. All hell broke loose as the other horsemen sped off with him.

The sound of the hunt diminished. Scheherazade waited a few moments, then she called, 'Dunyazad?'

There was no answer, just a rustling from the ground.

'Where are you? D?'

Scheherazade climbed down and looked into the other tree. Her sister was not there. She ran out through the small gate into the forest and found Dunyazad by the wall, gathering the fallen fruit into a basket. 'Father wouldn't want these ones lost,' she said. 'See? They are not spoiled.'

Scheherazade could see that Dunyazad was only making a show of getting on with domestic matters, and not very successfully hiding the light pouring from her face.

'Perhaps,' said Dunyazad, 'he will turn up again with jars of flowers.'

Scheherazade stamped her foot and hissed, 'Enough!' Jars of flowers were what the groom's family carried to a woman's house on the day of her wedding. 'That was the stupidest thing you've done!' said Scheherazade in a trembling voice. She became speechless.

'Oh, there you go again,' said Dunyazad. 'Stay on the ground. Live among the chickens. See what can be discovered scratching the same piece of ground.'

The clamour from within the forest continued but came no closer. When Jafar returned with news that the riders had ridden over Fatimah's hens, killing them all, neither of the sisters said what had happened by the fruit trees.

Later that day, servants from the palace came and stripped all the apricots from the trees in Jafar's little garden. All except one. They left one apricot hanging by itself. Then they put the fruit they had gathered into ornately woven baskets and disappeared. Jafar watched as the men took the fruit, saw how things lay, and bowed deeply at the honour.

3

Tears of the Moon

There came an evening not long afterwards when Scheherazade went with Jafar and Dunyazad to Ajedro's shop. Jafar walked upright and seemed less troubled than in recent days. When a man called out, 'Jafar, tell us a tale' – raising his cup of tea – Jafar motioned to Dunyazad. She went and sat in the talking-chair and began a tale, speaking as easily as petals on a flower open to the day, as easily as a bird returns to the nest.

At that moment, neither of the girls knew, and Jafar had not told them, that he had received a visit from the Principal of the Court, who had said that his youngest daughter had found favour with the king, and that it was requested that she join the queen's entourage. The girl's demeanour, fairness, and talent with words had been noted.

'I will tell a story that my father once told us,' said Dunyazad. 'It was many years ago on the Night of Nights, in the Days of Happiness, and I lay sleeping in the arms of my mother (on whom be peace). As we went through the woods we were woken by the light of the Moon. And I asked my father, is the Moon following us home? – for the Moon seemed to glide along beside us, just beyond the trees. The light bright, then dim, then bright again … My father replied, No. She wants to come with us, and she will even peep in at the window later, but she must stay where she is in the heavens.

'But, I said, she can sleep in our room. We can put a blanket on the floor.

'My father replied that there would indeed be room, but, no, she would not be allowed. For once, in the early days of the world, when the Moon was young, and the air was sweet, she went walking one night by the sea, and there, where the sea melts around the rockpools, she heard singing ...'

Scheherazade's mind went back to that night. She could see the glittering yellow tears flashing on the surface of the river. She did recall that it was *she* who had asked her father the question, 'is the moon following us home?', and *she* who had suggested they lay a blanket out for it. But then Dunyazad was the gifted one, so probably deserved to make the words her own. She felt irritated again, and desperately sad.

'... And those tears, shed by the Moon, become amber, a precious jewel, and if you are fortunate to find such a gift, and stare closely, in the amber you will see what the world holds for you in the tomorrows that lie waiting for us.'

Massoud Al Jazir applauded very loudly – big beefy handclaps – and leant over to whisper to Jafar. 'Such fine storytelling. Well done, my friend. My Amirah could learn a thing or two ...'

But not everyone was diverted. Scheherazade noticed a figure, a little beyond the light, resting with his back against a tree, and lost in thought. Or was he looking on with disapproval? The young man was Ishaq, the eldest son of a local woodcutting family, and Scheherazade and Dunyazad were friends with him and his sisters. Ishaq's mother had been good friends with their mother.

Ishaq had always been of quiet temper, especially since his own father had died. He was more inclined to be serious than to smile. And he was not smiling now. Since the visit of the king and the stripping of the apricot tree, Ishaq had not passed by the house as he usually might. Scheherazade had not seen him for days.

Having had enough of Dunyazad, and it looked as if she would now tell another story, Scheherazade stood and quietly walked over to stand with Ishaq. They greeted each other with a slight tilt of the head. 'My brother,' said Scheherazade. 'My sister,' said Ishaq.

Ishaq held a folded coat over his arm. Scheherazade took it and began to pick off strands of straw. 'It smells of elephant,' she said.

He plucked the coat back and put his nose to the fabric. 'No, definitely giraffe. I wasn't quick enough.'

'Can I take it and air it for you?'

'No, no,' said Ishaq. 'It will get worse treatment tomorrow. Thankyou.'

Ishaq had recently found employment in the palace. The king of a distant realm had sent a tribute to Tarquin. The gift included a small menagerie – a pygmy elephant, a giraffe, a monkey, a panther and other creatures. Ishaq, who had always tended the goats, and kept birds, had found work caring for these animals. Everyone in the village was surprised, for he had never shown an inclination to be part of the 'world of the palace'; but everyone agreed that he had done well for himself, especially on the day that the menagerie was put on display before the Tall Gates as a treat for the people. Ishaq had worn a new embroidered jacket, such as the ones worn in the court, and had led two small panthers on chains.

This jacket was the one that Ishaq now held onto tightly. Scheherazade looked as Ishaq folded it as small as he could manage, as if he were somehow ashamed of it.

'I will not stay,' he said. 'I must start early tomorrow.'

Dunyazad was now telling another tale – the story of Jasmine and the Magic Sandal, in which Jasmine outwits her wicked stepmother by tricking her clod of a father into running away with his beautiful but empty-headed stepdaughter.

'Goodnight,' said Ishaq. He walked off quickly.

Later, back home, Jafar sat them down and said that Dunyazad had been summoned to the court as a handmaid to Queen Amytis. She would leave in the morning.

'It is a great honour,' said Jafar.

Dunyazad burst into tears and ran out of the house, but Scheherazade knew that she was pleased. And Scheherazade suspected that Jafar must have known about the incident in the apricot tree, and had let

Dunyazad tell the stories that night in the village so that people would believe, once the news was generally known, that she had been taken to the queen's court because of her gift with words. Not for some shameful reason.

Later that night, Scheherazade, who had been simmering with anger, told her father about the hiding in the tree, the visit of the king, and about Dunyazad's boldness. He waved it away.

'I know of it,' said Jafar. 'Ishaq told me. He said he was trying to protect some new trees from being trampled by those hunters. He saw the king by the wall. He told me what he saw. I told him to make better use of his eyes. And not to spread gossip.'

Scheherazade's insides twisted. She could see now the reason why Ishaq had stopped greeting her, and why this night he had been a little more withdrawn. Had he been shamed by Jafar's rebuke? Had he seen Dunyazad and the king touch fingertips. Did he think badly of Dunyazad? Did he think badly of her?

In the morning, the Principal of the Court came with attendants and horses.

'I will bring fortune to this house,' said Dunyazad. Scheherazade was too upset to even roll her eyes.

But it seemed to be the case. Jafar, in a day or so, was restored to his old position at the palace and once more wrote dignified letters on behalf of the king and his advisors.

4

The Silver Room

In the palace, on a high floor of the main tower, there was a room, open only to the king and his most trusted advisors. It was called the Silver Room. There was just the one key to open the heavy door, and it was kept by Tarquin.

The room had a narrow, barred window overlooking the Great River, and the window was curtained. A few lanterns gave what little light was permitted. On one wall hung a portrait of King Zayn Al-Asnam, oil paint on cedar wood, and this was gashed and pecked where Tarquin had thrown a knife at it for target practice while thinking his thoughts.

In the centre of the room stood a long bench on which were laid several objects. All of them, in some manner, could show the future. Or so the king had been told when he bought them off the Scandinavian pirate Widsith, who brought them to Edessa.

There was a cylinder of gold, with strange markings. This was a seeing tube that could look into the future. It was dented where Tarquin had stomped on it repeatedly, for it tended to show nothing more than a dry inaccessible valley of red stone. There was a cage containing what looked like a mummified parrot. The parrot was fabled, every now and then, to speak words of clairvoyance. If the parrot had any messages for the living, it wasn't letting on. But Tarquin swore that the dead eyes of the parrot kept following him and so had the parrot turned to face the wall.

There were seeing stones from Iona – worthless because they only showed the inside of a cupboard somewhere; and there was a barnacle encrusted machine that foretold the positions of the planets and gave the times of eclipses, but this was only of passing interest to the king.

The main object of Tarquin's fascination was an amber necklace. Of all the objects, this one had given him keen revelations of the days to come. All he had to do was rub the amber, slowly, until it grew warm, and in the dimness of the room an image of some future event would become visible in the face of the jewel. Sometimes the image was misty and unfocussed; and sometimes crystal clear, but still dreamlike.

The amber necklace had shown Tarquin his victory over the Grassland Kingdom. He rode out confidently to claim it – something that he hadn't really considered doing until the necklace laid it before him. The necklace had revealed the outcome of several battles, the movements of enemies, and the location of fugitives. So far, so good. But one day the necklace showed him the queen looking deeply into someone's eyes. Tarquin's heart jumped with pleasure, for he assumed that *he* was the recipient of her glances. But a suspicion stole upon him that it was someone else she looked at with longing, for her eyes seemed sad and troubled.

Tarquin instructed attendants to keep a secret eye upon Amytis. And when that revealed nothing, stung by what seemed to be her faithlessness, he set his own eyes to look on other women. In reality, the queen had no intention of looking into anyone else's eyes, until she felt the growing chill from her husband. His suspicion was like the first red autumn leaf. And then the falling leaves were everywhere.

The images of victory in battle gave way to images of warriors gathering in caves, and furtive figures looking closely at a map of Edessa. Someone was looking at a plan of the palace. One image showed a man cutting his hand with a knife in a blood-pledge. These images came more rapidly now; or else it was that the king looked into the necklace more frequently. Even in the middle of the night.

The guards at the door to the Silver Room had to be replaced every few days, for their nerves began to fray waiting for the king to leap up the stairs like a demon from a tomb.

One day Tarquin saw images that confirmed all the rumours he had heard: he saw a flying carpet racing across the desert. And on it was a figure, slight in build, and wearing strange garments, like the assassins from the Orient who knew how to steal into secret fortresses. The carpet came closer. The figure clutched a sword, it carried a hessian bag. Tarquin strained to see who the figure might be, but clouds of black dust blew across the vison. The image was replaced by one of Zayn Al-

Asnam laughing, his hands bouncing up and down on his stomach.

Extra guards were stationed along the palace walls and patrols were increased.

*

Tarquin had had on the surface, a pleasant morning on that day when Scheherazade and Dunyazad were hiding in the apricot tree. The riding, if not the hunting, had got his blood racing. His tongue still savoured the apricots he had eaten, though he had largely forgotten the girl who had handed him the fruit. The daughter of one of the scribes, he was told. But his mind, as usual, was set on the Great Game with Zayn Al-Asnam, facing him as if across a ghostly chessboard.

Without changing from his hunting gear Tarquin hurried to the Silver Room. The guards by the door slammed their spears smartly to the floor and stood rigid, their nostrils flaring.

Tarquin hurried past, turned the key, and entered the room. He drew a dagger and flung it at the tip of Zayn Al-Asnam's nose. It stuck there. Satisfied, Tarquin moved to the table. The itch was upon him. He picked up the necklace and held it, counting each piece of amber through his fingers, with his eyes closed, until he settled on the one that seemed 'right'. The room was sufficiently dark. He began to caress the amber until he felt warmth and a tingling in his fingers, then he held the jewel up to his face.

The image today was clear. There was the assassin riding upon a flying carpet, bathed in moonlight. The figure seemed to rest hunched over in thought, wrapped in a dark cloak, or perhaps seized with deadly emotions. Tarquin was so engrossed that he felt as if *he* were flying alongside the carpet, caught in the wake of the rider, and drawing closer; but no matter how much he stared, or turned the jewel to one side (when he pointed the jewel down, it revealed the Great River below), he could not move around or get past the figure to see their face. But no matter who it was, the destination was now clear. Beneath them was the kingdom of Edessa. The assassin rode on the moonlight towards the palace.

But now, something new was happening. The carpet dropped out of the sky and was flying above the forest, descending to the level of the trees. It slowed, next to a wall, over which apricot trees grew. Even though it was moonlit, Tarquin knew it at once as the place where he had paused that morning, where the young girl was hiding. The assassin flew over the apricot trees and disappeared into the courtyard beyond.

The amber went dark. Tarquin lowered the necklace and, gasping, began to write a description of the things he had seen.

After finishing, he turned to the motionless parrot. 'And do you have anything to add?'

The parrot held its peace.

'I thought not. That girl, or perhaps her father,' continued Tarquin, 'they are in league with that rogue Al-Asnam …'

He wondered if the apricots he had eaten had been poisoned and made himself sick up in the corner of the room.

He considered having the girl and her father executed. But the trick, he knew, was rather to play them, and use them to bring the key rebels, the important players, out of the shadows. The rider on the carpet must be captured and his commanders discovered. It would give him the necessary reason to invade and shame Zayn Al-Asnam, and then imprison him.

That day Tarquin gave commands. He had the apricot tree stripped of fruit, to see how the rebels responded. But nothing came of this. No-one blinked. No-one made a move. He then arranged for the girl and her father to be brought to the palace, making the request seem innocent, even benevolent. Keep your enemies in striking distance is what his grandfather Henry had counselled. But no matter how much he had the father and daughter spied upon, they neither of them put a foot wrong. On the surface, they seemed innocent. Watchers were placed in the forest to observe the other daughter of Jafar, to see if she met with anyone, to see if her behaviour suggested a conspiracy. But nothing out of the ordinary was revealed.

'If you have any ideas, now is the time,' said Tarquin to the dead parrot.

The main result of Tarquin's strategy was that Queen Amytis grew secretly angry that Tarquin was furtively watching the new girl in the court. He seemed to keep his eyes upon her at every turn. And so her eyes, and her heart, wandered to someone else, just as the necklace foretold.

Ajedro's Luck

Since her father and sister were more at the palace than not, Scheherazade went to visit Ajedro every other evening after work, bringing him bread, and sharing a meal with him. She went one day and found that her life was to take another turn for the worse. It happened this way.

Under Queen Amytis, a garden of culture had blossomed in the palace. She often invited poets and storytellers, musicians and dancers to the spacious rooms of the New Palace. Scribes and illustrators, artists, were kept busy. It was Amytis who had arranged for the public display of the menagerie. The queen also encouraged local craftspeople. Perhaps on a word from Dunyazad, or so it was supposed, the queen visited Ajedro's bookshop and purchased, in a morning, an amount of books equal to what Jafar had bought in all the time he had known Ajedro. And most of the objects and curios.

When Scheherazade visited in the evening, the shop seemed to have been looted. But Ajedro was happy, and villagers came up and shook his hand. Ajedro ordered food and the two of them ate a small feast in the open air. He declared to Scheherazade that he would take the opportunity to re-stock his shop, and planned to make a journey over the Great River in search of new treasures.

'I will go first through the Old Kingdom,' he said. 'There are villages and towns at the edge of the desert that trade in the oldest books and oldest scrolls. Your father will be pleased. I will bring him a few surprises. And perhaps some stories that your sister can use to amuse the queen. Did you ever hear of the Cave of the Five Golden Cups?'

Scheherazade said that she had not.

'Ibn al-Muqaffa writes about it. He said he had found the cave – but then lost the map! Can you believe it? What would you say if I told you that the cave holds the *last* of the Five Golden Cups that gives to the one who drinks from it the power of charmed speech? I think it must be somewhere up in the foothills of the Zagros Mountains.'

'You are going to the Zagros Mountains?' said Scheherazade, wide-eyed.

'Only the foothills. Don't worry. I'll stay where it is safe … It would be a rare find, though. Your father would like a drink from that cup, I think – give him a chance to win in Samarkand and beat old Massoud (don't tell your father I said that!).'

Ajedro finished off the hummus and kept speaking.

'And they say there are wonderful stories written in a golden book, in the very same cave. Your sister could hold the court spellbound with those. Unheard stories. Not that she needs it, of course. Though, you never know. No-one has an endless supply of stories,' he ended with a kind of grim look.

'Where is the cave?' asked Scheherazade.

'No-one knows. It is said to lie in the foothills near the Shrine of Ersa, which I will visit and make a little offering in return for my good fortune.'

Ersa was a daughter of the moon, whose main duty in the world was to sprinkle dew in the hours before dawn.

'And this little one might benefit from the journey,' said Ajedro, pointing to where Tonto sat up on the awning of the shop, turning in circles, wringing his hands.

'What is wrong with him?' said Scheherazade. 'Is he unwell?'

'Ever since … you remember when those animals were paraded in front of the Tall Gates? Your Ishaq was leading the panthers. And we all wanted to see the elephant and Tonto sat on my shoulder? I think he has fallen in love with the little lady monkey. He sat up when she appeared and looked stunned. He was quite taken with her. He went all bashful.'

'I suppose he has no memory of his own kind,' said Scheherazade, holding up a pistachio, which the monkey ignored.

'He tells me nothing, do you?!' said Ajedro, calling out. 'Never a word! Poor thing.'

'I could look after him,' said Scheherazade. 'While you travel?'

'No. I need someone to share my thoughts with, and he doesn't cost much for a travelling companion.'

Ajedro left the next day and had been gone for a few days, when, to add to her loneliness, Ishaq also left the village. His sister gave Scheherazade the news. Ishaq had gone to look for work in the north-eastern forests far from Edessa, she said. He would establish himself, then return to take the family to live with him there.

He had not even said farewell.

Scheherazade spent the evening crying in the empty house.

6

The Terror Begins

Scheherazade hurried through the forest. It was before sunrise and the wood-doves and pheasants were awake, singing in the grey light. Cyclamen shone like melting snow in the wet undergrowth. A peacock let out a mournful screech from a branch over the path.

As Scheherazade left the hamlet where their home was, she began to feel again that strange emptiness, the feeling of being followed, which had started, she felt, even before Dunyazad went to the palace. The feeling had grown worse now that she had to leave the quiet house and make her own way to Aunt Paribanou's bakery. She had never felt uneasy before in the forest, where she had always lived. She wondered if it was just loneliness – her father away, Ajedro gone, Ishaq gone – that made her feel this way.

The path through the forest ran up to the walls of the bakery, and to a small door for which she had a key. Scheherazade was glad when she got there.

As quietly as she could she went into the enclosed yard. She whispered to the dog, who, knowing her footsteps, flapped his ear and lay still with his paws crossed. 'Just me, Bacbouc,' she said, warming her hands underneath his large ears. 'No-one else.' She lifted and pressed the dog's soft head to her chest and felt comforted.

7

Scheherazade undid the latch on the chicken coop. Croaking hens fell out and began to peck the ground and walk over the dog. She slid back the heavy plank that held the main gates closed and dragged the gates open. She avoided looking into the dark forest and turned quickly towards the shelter of the oven house. A small bat, soft as soot, flicked out.

There were two fires to be lit: the hearth fire, and the large oven. Scheherazade stirred up the ash pit and found a few embers from the previous day. She blew on these, fed them bits of straw. In the shifting light her shadow began to dance on the wall. When both fires were set, she planted a kettle in the small hearth and hurried outside. There was a ring of stones in the courtyard and she started a fire there. This was harder because of the damp earth, but soon this one was also burning. There was no standing still now.

As if knowing that an extra pair of hands were needed, Maruf the timber-merchant walked in from the forest and hailed her in a quiet voice. They bowed to each other.

'Good morning, O my uncle,' said Scheherazade. 'You are here early!'

He put down his axe. 'Early is best. Let me throw wood scraps on this. You run on. Mistress Paribanou must be wanting her morning drink.'

Ibrahim and Sulayman, Maruf's sons came in, and they warmed themselves by the fire. Maruf ground coffee in a hand mill.

There was now a general stir in the forest. Cries echoed back and forth through the darkness as the boatmen left their homes and walked the tracks to the river. Near the gate came the *pud-pud, pud-pud* of hooves. Al-Haddar, who owned and traded mules, walked in, dispensing greetings, and stood by the fire with his thumbs hitched into his belt. Al-Kuzuz, the one-eyed mule driver and Al-Haddar's labourer, busied himself watering the mules beyond the gate. Scheherazade had already toasted day-old bread in a pan with a little oil and passed this around. Al-Haddar threw some coins in the jar and helped himself.

Scheherazade made a mint tea for her Aunt and took the rest of the hot water to Maruf who threw in the coffee grounds. Scheherazade was glad that Maruf was there, for all these little tasks should have been carried out by two, which had been the case until Dunyazad's sudden elevation.

The small set of stairs that ran up to Paribanou's quarters creaked as she went up. On hearing this, Bacbouc let out a few low barks: knowing that his mistress would now be waking, it paid to be seen to be about one's business.

Scheherazade knocked and took in the glass of tea.

'You are a good girl,' said Paribanou.

Scheherazade set the tea down and placed a cushion behind her aunt's shoulders. She half opened one of the louvres. On the Great River, an early boat was heading downstream. From here she could see the palace and wondered what waited for Dunyazad this day. Reciting ghazals, entertaining the children of the court ladies, talking with the queen? The high walls of the palace had just caught the eastern light.

'And does Dunyazad enjoy her work?' asked Paribanou, sipping tea.

'I have not yet heard,'

'She has a way with words. She will do well.'

But Paribanou had done nothing in the past week or so that looked like hiring another girl or boy from the village to bear the load of small tasks that now fell to Scheherazade. Perhaps, thought Scheherazade, she has no faith in Dunyazad's talents and expects her back in due time to keep making the loaves.

As she hurried back down the stairs to the yard, the trumpets for the opening of the city gates sounded, the reedy noise drifting over the forest. Maruf and his sons went on their way.

It was only when the first loaves came out of the oven that Scheherazade heard the horns, the five blasts, to signal that the king would be hunting.

Scheherazade hurried to speak with Paribanou. 'O, my aunt, the king is hunting. I must put our hens away.'

'Go, go, you have time. Tch! I will see to things here. Be quick!'

Scheherazade ran through the myrtle grove back to the house. The hens were safely away when the horses approached the back wall as they had done on the day she hid in the apricot tree. But Scheherazade felt sick and ashamed at the memory and hid in the shadows of the house. Through a crack in the closed louvre, she looked out. A rider stopped, dismounted, and handed their hunting spear to an attendant. Pulling off gloves, they walked into the yard (she had not closed the gate in coming through).

It was the king. She stepped back, away from the light.

Tarquin looked around, then sent his gaze quickly up into the branches of the apricot trees. And further, up into the sky, craning his head back. He looked at the house, at the flat roof, then the slatted window. If she had been standing in the light, he might have seen her. But she could see a heaviness of anger and pain in his face. A woodman, who did not look at all familiar, hurried into the yard and spoke to the king in a low voice, and Scheherazade froze, for she was sure that the words, 'the second daughter of Jafar' had been spoken. The woodman bowed quickly, an almost military style bow, and hurried away.

Tarquin then made a strange gesture. As if he knew that someone was inside the house looking at him, he pointed at his eye, as if to say, 'I am watching you'. He then returned to the path, wrapped himself in a plain travelling cloak and mounted a new horse. He covered his face in a scarf. Two other men, dressed in similar fashion, their features cloaked, rode up, and the three sped off. Scheherazade could hear no other sounds, apart from the wind in the trees.

She carefully walked into the yard and stepped out onto the forest path. Suddenly, men on horseback charged down the path, sounding their horns. The hunt was not over as she had thought. She feared for a moment that they had come for her, for spying on the king. But the riders yelled at her to move. A pack of dogs swirled around and past her like starlings over a barn. The hunters passed by, but they could be heard zig-zagging through the forest, their horns startling the air. Scheherazade abandoned the path for safety-sake and returned to the bakery through the bushes and undergrowth.

Then the hunt – if it had been a hunt – ended, with no animals taken, except for all of Mozir's goats. Some riders milled around. One or two men rode into the yard and bought bread. After a while, the horsemen rode away in stony silence.

Around mid-afternoon, as business resumed, a man hurried in with the news. The king had secretly returned to the palace from the forest and surprised the queen in the arms of one of the poets. The queen and the poet had been beheaded. Their bodies had been hung from the gates.

Paribanou pressed a handkerchief to her face and hurried indoors.

'It will be war with Akkadia,' said a man. The courtyard emptied.

Scheherazade turned and washed her hands in a jar of water, shook them dry and hurried out of the yard. She turned down the path that led to the city. But someone hurried towards her. It was Sulayman.

'My sister, where are you going?'

'To the palace.'

He shook his head and came close. 'No. Don't go there.'

'But what about my father? What about Dunyazad?'

He shook his head. 'I don't know. There are soldiers everywhere. Go home. Alright?'

But Scheherazade was already thinking about Ajedro and her father's words to seek him out.

As she thought this, the smell of smoke drifted over the forest. Sulayman waited no longer and hurried away.

Scheherazade saw that the smoke was coming from the direction of Ajedro's village. She turned down a narrow path, one that she and Dunyazad used to walk. Again, there was the feeling of being watched. To shake off the feeling she hurried down twisting side paths and hid in undergrowth until the feeling vanished.

Smoke was drifting through the trees and grew thicker as she ran on. She covered her mouth to breathe and had to back away. She retraced her steps and walked the long way round to approach the village through an orchard. She came to the small square, but couldn't go any further. Flames poured out of Ajedro's shop, and soldiers with firebrands stood before it.

The Journey

*

Ibn al-Muqaffa has written about the Five Golden Cups … The first cup was devoured by a dragon, and it received thus the gift of elegant speech. Dragons had long talked, but only of dull, violent matters; when the golden cup was consumed (and that dragon in turn consumed by other dragons) dragons more generally became dealers in riddles and wordplay. The second cup was taken to Samarkand and found its way into the hands of a dentist who used small pieces of it to fill the teeth of his clients. As a result, the people of Samarkand became great storytellers, and the Festival of Tales is the highpoint of their calendar. The third cup went to Palestine in the hands of a gnostic sect; the fourth was removed to Atlantis … It is said that the fifth was left undisturbed in a cave in the foothills of the Zagros Mountains – but don't believe it. The people of that land will tell you anything!

from The Nights of Abu Nuwas

1

The Shrine of Ersa

five days later

The Shrine of Ersa had been built to keep the desert away from a small village near the foothills of the Zagros Mountains. Families from the Greek lands had once lived there, and as the sand stole into their orchards and weakened the roots of the trees, they built the shrine and invited the goddess to dwell with them and put forth her influence. The Greeks were now long gone and the orchard with them. But the statue of the goddess remained in her shrine, which was a simple building of whitewashed stone, surrounded by drifting level sand. Nearby stood a tree of old bones.

For reasons not fully understood, the inside of the shrine remained cool and moist. Travellers would stop there and take in the refreshing air. Women who could not have a child visited and asked for the goddess's influence with her mother, the moon.

The shrine was three days travel from Edessa and the Great River. Scheherazade made it there in less than two days.

The shrine's cool interior was a relief after the desert wastes. Scheherazade entered, and straightaway fell on her knees before the small figure of Ersa, who was carved from a kind of blue marble. In front of the goddess was a discoloured metal bowl. Scheherazade carried a water bag and slung this off her shoulder. She poured out what was left into the bowl. She knelt back, her hands lifted in prayer. Her fingers touched her mouth – her lips were cracked – her breath was ragged.

'O goddess,' she said. 'Open to me the river of your mercy, and water me with full streams, from the springs of your grace, from the depths of your loving-kindness. Thank you that you have guided my feet and have brought me here in safety. Look upon me the smallest of your children.'

There came a soft scraping sound.

'Speak,' said Ersa. The voice was cracked and old. 'Tell me your troubles.'

'O goddess, I don't know if you know, but the queen has been killed ...'

'Oh, yes, we all heard that. Everything is in turmoil.'

'My sister, who served in her court, came home that same night. But ...'

Scheherazade's face wrinkled and tears splashed on the marble floor.

'Your tears are my gift,' said Ersa. 'My tears water the forests at night, and the stones of the mountain before dawn. Speak on.'

'She came home, but ... my father who is a scribe is held prisoner in the palace ... They say he is in the Red Room.'

Ersa said, 'Oh ...' then, 'that is no good.'

'The guard who escorted my sister home said it was to guarantee obedience.'

'Puzzling,' said Ersa. 'Had your father done anything to offend the king? Or had your sister?'

'No. She went there to tell stories in the queen's court, and she said it was a cold and dreadful place. That they looked on her with disdain for no reason, except perhaps that she was not fair-skinned. And she said that the queen said nothing to her, but looked on her with anger. She tried to tell everyone a story, and her voice dried up. She thinks that the queen saw her as some kind of spy, put there by the king ...

'Then the day after the queen was killed, there was a proclamation. The king said that he was open to marrying someone whose loyalty and faithfulness were beyond reproach. He merely asked that the woman should have the ability to amuse him with a story on their wedding night, for the queen used to soothe him by telling him stories. And if he wasn't amused ...'

'Speak on,' said Ersa.

'My father has a friend, Massoud Al Jazir, who is loyal to the king. His daughter, Amirah, is perhaps the most gifted of the young storytellers. He put her name forward, confident that she would easily divert the king, and the wedding was contracted, and in the evening the king asked her to tell a story. I believe that she told a story never heard before, about a Princess who falls in love with a young street beggar named Al'Adin. He struggles to support his mother, but one day finds a magic lamp in a deep cave, and from it comes a long-imprisoned *djinn* that befriends Al'Adin, and through trials he becomes worthy of the Princess. And they find happiness. And I hear there was a battle with an evil wizard, and a magical procession. There's more. But I'm not saying it right.'

'It sounds just the thing,' said Ersa with a small chuckle.

'No!' said Scheherazade. 'Amirah was executed in the morning. And her father died on hearing the news.'

The goddess was quiet for a long moment.

Scheherazade could not stop her tears. 'He was my father's friend.'

'This king is not like his father, Montague,' said Ersa eventually. 'Now, *there* was a king ... Speak on ... child.'

'That day, no-one proposed their daughter. So the king issued a list, giving the names of the young women who must marry the king. And the storytellers gathered in trepidation and gave to each daughter a story, their best stories. They have so far tried the stories of Sinbad, and Ali Baba and the Forty Thieves – thinking that stories like these would regale the king. One after the next the women have all been executed.'

'And you have fled here because your name is on the list?' said Ersa.

'No. I am not on the list. But my sister is the ninth name.'

'Well, *you* have come here? Could she not have come with you, and the two of you hidden in the mountains?'

'They threaten the villages. If a young woman does not appear as demanded, her family and village suffer.'

'Of course ... I am glad that I am old,' said Ersa. 'So what has happened that you are here?'

'I went and stood in the forest and wept, and then I knew what I should do.'

'Yes. And go on ...'

'There is a man who owns a bookshop in the nearby village, my father's good friend. He told me once of a cave, where there is a golden cup that gives to whoever drinks from it the power of telling stories – and that there are stories written on leaves of gold, that my sister could tell, in a kind of book. I think she just needs one, a really good one ...'

'A better one than Sinbad?' murmured the goddess.

'... one that she can use to ... stay the hand of the king. And stories to help her survive all the other nights to follow. So I vowed to leave straightaway and find this cave, but ...'

'But?'

'I went to the house of a friend, to ask her to be with my sister while I was gone, but something happened on the way. As I went through the forest, Maruf the timber merchant was walking a nearby path, and because I had stopped to cry, he met up with me where the paths joined and asked me if I knew that someone was secretly watching me. Someone from the palace. Perhaps an agent of the king.'

'This is like a travelling storyteller,' said Ersa. 'What happened then?'

2

Escape to the Old Kingdom

'Walk with me,' said Maruf. 'Here, wipe your eyes.'

Scheherazade fell in step with Maruf. As they passed through a thicket, he said, 'Where are you walking to?'

'I'm going to Ishaq's house.'

'But, he is gone ...'

'I must ask his mother to look in on Dunyazad, because I have to leave the forest, I have to ...'

'A little softer,' said Maruf.

'I have to find Ajedro ...'

'Why? To tell him that his house is burned down?'

Scheherazade began to tell him of her intention to find Ajedro.

As she spoke, Maruf took a mandarin from his pocket, peeled it and shared it.

'No more. Say no more,' said Maruf uncertainly. 'It is best that I know little of your plans.' He brushed pips from his beard and spoke through his fingers, 'Come to the yard after you visit Ishaq's family. Pick flowers on the way. Walk idly. Come in through the yard, not the house. And don't go home.'

'Ever since Dunyazad went to the palace,' said Scheherazade, 'even before, I have felt that I was being followed. And I thought it was just loneliness. But now you say that there is a watcher.'

'Yes,' affirmed Maruf in a quiet voice. 'Wearing a woodman's coat, so that he blends in with the trees. But no woodman that I know.'

Maruf walked on and Scheherazade went to visit Ishaq's mother, hoping that her heart beating loudly could not be heard.

She came away after a few minutes with a small gift of dried figs. She walked to Maruf's dwelling, gathering odd wildflowers as she walked, swatting at long grass with a stick. The forest was quiet.

The sheds of Maruf's business were a chessboard of scattered buildings, and piles of timber rising like small forts.

She walked into the yard. Maruf's voice called softly to her, 'Come through here. Do not speak.'

Maruf stood in the shadows of an open-ended building which held some handcarts and tree-work tools. She walked in, glancing behind her. Maruf opened a door into a small room that adjoined the house. It was filled with baskets, rope, wet-weather gear.

'I will leave you here for a moment,' he said. 'Put on these spare work clothes. They used to belong to Haroum. They will fit you well. This jacket has a hood. Put your outer clothes into this sack that you can sling over your shoulder. See, I have here a small pouch with olives and bread. I'm putting it into the sack. Put those figs in too, and put the wildflowers in. Leave no trace that you came through here. When you are ready, knock twice on this door that I am going through.' Maruf disappeared into the house. In the gloom, Scheherazade changed into the clothes. She took off her veil and put it into one of the pockets. She found a piece of cloth and tied up her hair.

She could hear words through the door – Maruf and his wife talking. 'You are bringing misfortune into the house, husband. First the mother dies, now the father is imprisoned, the youngest girl is on a death list. Bad luck will come to this one soon, mark my words, and through her, into our house …'

'Mine isn't one of your Roman gods,' came the reply.

'Well, she doesn't come into the kitchen …'

'Dearest, she is outside. And if anyone asks, say that you thought you heard her pass through the yard, as she has done before, and nothing more …'

Scheherazade took a breath and knocked twice. Maruf came back in. He led her back to the place where the handcarts were. She noticed that there were many bundles of sticks piled up inside the entrance, and Ibrahim and Sulayman were standing there. They looked at Scheherazade and then looked at the ground. I must wear misfortune like a veil, she thought.

'Come close,' said Maruf. 'There is a fair-skinned rogue in the woods, watching our sister here. I know not why. And nor does she. I will walk from here down the village path, and see if I can surprise him, draw his eye. I'll talk of weather and woodcraft. While I do this, the three of you will shoulder your burdens and take these bundles of sticks to the charcoal maker. They are not heavy, my daughter. The easiness is in the balancing.'

'And in doing it ten times before sunrise,' said Ibrahim.

'I carry sacks of flour every day,' said Scheherazade.

Maruf nodded. 'So, keep your hood on, and your head down. Walk second. My boys, there are plenty more of these bundles to deliver, so, come back and carry on the task. Make no mention of any of this. Talk if you must, or sing, but ask her no questions.'

Scheherazade hoisted the bundle of sticks onto her shoulders and went second of three.

Maruf walked into the yard without any further talk. He strolled out of the yard. A few moments later he could be heard hailing someone.

'Come,' said Sulayman. He led them out and they turned out through the same path that Maruf had taken but walking the opposite direction. Scheherazade did not look up but heard Maruf a short way off talking noisily with someone. She looked at the path beneath her feet and walked with the weight of wood and sharp sticks pressing into her back.

*

Five hours later, after following small tracks, and always looking behind, the forest ended. The land fell. It was a point where the Great River ran over descending steps of rocks, breaking apart into small cataracts and shallowing into wide channels and islands. It picked up other tributaries at this point – including the River Korsakov that ferried silt and mud from the Caspian Ranges. This landscape, though not many miles from her home, was completely unfamiliar: spreading marshland, bending papyrus. It was not an empty land. Many people walked the tracks and bridges that formed a wide path along the western edge of the waterway. Traces of evening were starting to show. Squadrons of birds were coasting over the river. The air was tinted smokey orange and green.

Scheherazade came to a place on the river where barges crossed. After waiting for nearly an hour she found a ride on one. On board, she felt a desperate urge to jump back off and not cross the river, for the barge seemed to sit too low in the water when she stepped on with the others. She was sure there were too many people, and some moaned in fear as the water lapped over the wood. But there was no capsize, just a gripping silence as the passengers swallowed their panic.

Scheherazade remembered her father's tale of the ferryman who carried the souls of the dead across the Last River. In her mind the image had always taken the shape of a single person sitting in a boat, while the far shore, crowded with silent spectral figures, swam out of a bleak fog; but now the reality was the barge, thick with silent passengers, evening mist on the water, moving towards a flat treeless emptiness.

Safe on the other side, the passengers hurried away from each other.

Aimlessly walking, Scheherazade heard a voice that she knew. It was Al-Haddar, his voice clear above the braying of his mules. He looked at her suspiciously when she came up and caught his eye and he looked away, as if embarrassed to know her. He kept up a brief show of haggling with the people who were desperate and willing to pay whatever he asked for his animals.

Scheherazade felt that Al-Haddar's coolness could not be helped: the more that people knew of Jafar's fate, of Dunyazad's place on the list, the more they would look on her as the child of an unfortunate family and keep their distance. Maruf's wife had said as much. And Al-Haddar's attention seemed to be fixed on the large amounts of silver he could command for even the poorest beast. But after a few minutes he called for Al-Kuzuz to keep up the bargaining and turned to her.

'What are you doing here?'

She told him that she was looking for Ajedro. 'Father said to find him if things turned bad.'

'Things *have* turned bad, but I don't know what help the old man can give you.' Al-Haddar walked away and then walked back. 'Go home, my daughter. Paribanou will take care of you? Won't she? No? How on earth do you plan to find Ajedro?'

'How do I get to the shrine of Ersa?' said Scheherazade. 'He said he would visit there.'

Al-Haddar sucked his teeth. 'Ersa? Blessed be the goddess. Is that where he is? That shrine, that village, is two or three days from here over the desert. Maybe four of five if you plan to walk.'

'If I have to,' she said.

'No, no. You cannot walk.' Al-Haddar made a face, clacked his teeth, and came to a decision. 'I have sold ten mules to that train there,' he said, pointing. 'Cacik is the captain of the train. And I will ask him to let you ride. I will pay him for his trouble.'

'O, my uncle,' said Scheherazade.

'Peace. He is taking some merchants through the Old Kingdom, but you will only be with him two nights. This coming night and the next. He puts on the pace. On the second morning from now you will have to make your own way. His road continues east, but you will bear south along the path that runs through the ruins of Mandab. It's a donkey's leg, but in a way quicker. And you cannot walk.'

'I have nothing to give you in return.'

'Then we need waste no time haggling. Come with me, quick. He leaves now and will journey for a few hours before stopping for a short night.'

They walked together. 'And if you travel on alone,' said Al-Haddar, 'do not sleep in the open – do you hear? Find a ruined temple and sleep on top of a pillar, or on a ledge, or on the altar if you have to. Climb even if it makes your fingers bleed but keep off the ground at night. Snakes, hyenas ... not to mention those merchants, don't take gifts from them. I will pay Cacik all that is necessary. You don't need favours from those merchants, and they don't need favours from you. Do you understand me?' He took out a small purse and emptied it of all except a few coins. 'Take this – it is a little silver. Do not say anything. And don't say who you got it from. Say a dead aunt. And what else? Yes, when you get to the shrine do not wander into the Zagros Mountains.'

'Is the shrine close to the mountains?' asked Scheherazade, clearing her throat.

'*Yes*, it is. It is right at the very foot of the mountains. And I don't need to tell you the mountains are stiff with *djinns*, and evil magic.'

He had no need to tell her these things.

*

The night and the following day were uneventful. The mule train made its steady progress a little north of east. Cacik, the captain of the mule train, had a way of making people feel at home, making sure there were never any uncomfortable silences. He would speak about how good mules were. How well-built and certain. And very intelligent in a quiet way. Many people shunned a mule, he said, but they were stronger than a donkey; and not as highly strung as a horse. A mule was less susceptible to the diseases that can take away a horse or a donkey. A mule was the best of both worlds. He could talk all day about a mule.

The train was one of the last to travel that way before the great heat of summer came on. Even now, in early spring, the heat and light left your eyes aching and you longed for shade, for the softness of trees. There were people on the same trail, struggling with the unexpected travail of walking in the hot wastes. Scheherazade was ashamed when looks and glances came her way from families barely able to walk in a straight line, while she rode along unburdened. But they looked as if they had not even the energy to condemn.

The night came and passed quickly. Scheherazade slept within the circle of animals until a bright light brayed at her, and she woke, looking straight into a dazzling moon. She did not go back to sleep after that.

The moon set, and before the sun rose, at the point where the southern track appeared, the mule train continued on its way. Cacik gave Scheherazade a waterbag and briefly farewelled her, his face just visible.

'Al-Haddar said you are visiting the Shrine of Ersa and the Ten Villages. Go that way. It is a broken road, but firm underfoot. You will feel the stones under your feet. Do not wander. You should have bought yourself a mule. Better than a donkey. Well. Goodbye.'

Scheherazade began to walk. The track in front of her was like something you see when you squeeze your eyes shut. But it came clear as the sky brightened and the sun rose. Scheherazade found herself walking an old road through blown sand, red stone ridges, and alongside a dry riverbed, in a pure silence broken only by her too-loud footsteps. Sheherazade walked half a day and before noon entered the ruins of the city of Mandab.

She had made good time, and because of that, in her haste, she made a mistake. She decided to continue on the path, even though there was nothing ahead but a dull haze that seemed to promise shadows and temperate light. But the heat did not diminish and she took a beating from it. She stumbled on, and realised that at some point she had left the path and the air was suddenly a misty red, and not cool. She could see only a few paces in front of her, but the horizon was gone. The sudden fright of it drained her. Her legs gave way and she found herself lying on the ground in the quiet redness, watching the red dust settle on her hands and clothes. She clung on to the waterbag as one clutches a pillow in a nightmare. Eventually the fear broke up a little. She righted herself and took sips of water until she felt ready to stand once again.

The red mist melted away, revealing clear blue skies. A call from a camel made her stand up. A small caravan with tents was resting only a stone's throw from her, as if placed there by the hand of an angel. She shook the sand off her clothes, and walked towards the caravan, desperate for shade. From a tent, as she approached, a young man with a fine dark complexion stepped out.

'Are you a mirage?' he said.

Scheherazade said, 'No, sir.' They bowed to each other. Scheherazade gave the traditional greeting and the man gave a clumsy rendition of the same. 'I am learning your ways, and happy to be taught. My name is Achmed.'

'My name is Scheherazade, daughter of Jafar, and of Marjanah, on whom be peace.'

Another man came from the tent. Scheherazade saw that he wore a uniform marking him as one of Tarquin's senior guards. Her mouth seized up. Achmed, however, politely asked this man to attend to their guest and Scheherazade was taken to a small tent. She was brought water and fruit and a dish of rice with almonds. The man attending her said his name was Iram bin Ad, and told her that her host was none other than Prince Achmed, Son of the Sultan of the Indies, travelling in the land as a guest of King Tarquin. 'I serve him on behalf of King Tarquin and Queen Amytis.'

Scheherazade realised that this man knew nothing of the recent events in the kingdom.

Scheherazade was left alone to eat and rest. A short time later the Prince came to the tent and sat with Scheherazade.

'We are returning from the Zagros Mountains,' he said conversationally. 'I have been searching for an extraordinary treasure.'

'Did you find it?' said Scheherazade, her interest kindling.

'I think that depends on the one who will receive it as a gift,' laughed the Prince. 'You see, I have two brothers (I am the youngest of three, and so the one with the least cares) and they have both fallen in love with our cousin, a lady named Nouronnihar. Our uncle decreed that the brother who brings back the most extraordinary treasure as a gift for his daughter will be allowed to make an offer of marriage. And my brothers insisted I join the quest, just in case our cousin fell for me while they were absent. And I believe I have found just the gift ...'

'What is it?" asked Scheherazade.

'A magical tent,' he said. His eyes twinkled as he took from his pocket a folded square of fabric, no bigger than a napkin. 'It folds up and slips into your pocket; but when you pitch it, you discover that it holds within it a small army, and horses, they said. I think the villagers in the Zagros Mountains will be very happy with what I paid them!'

'Did you not pitch the tent first to see that there was such an army inside?' asked Scheherazade.

'No, they said the army only appears when the need arises. At all other times it looks like an ordinary piece of cloth.'

'Then it is very magical,' said Scheherazade. They both laughed.

'I will let you rest, but we must break camp within the hour. The storm has slowed our progress. Do you need to travel with us? You will be welcome. Perhaps safer.'

'No. I am very grateful for your hospitality, but I have to go south. I am visiting the Shrine of Ersa.'

'I will ask my aide what he knows of the journey, if that is helpful.' The Prince asked her no other questions, rose, bowed, and Scheherazade rested in the shade of the tent until there was a noise of activity and the creaky wheezing of camels.

The Prince's aide returned, bringing food and the waterbag, filled.

'If you will go south,' said Iram bin Ad, 'the time for travel is now. Follow the road, such as it is, and you will strike the ruins of a small town. All being well, you will be there by sunset. There is a well in that village, the water is drinkable, and there is an abandoned temple – a raised place where you should sleep. The shrine of Ersa and the villages of the foothills are three hours beyond, but you do not want to walk through the night. Wait till the early morning.'

Scheherazade asked him to thank the Prince.

The man bowed, and soon the caravan was tufts of red dust to the north.

The caravan had seemed to her like something from a different world or a different time – a time where the queen was not dead (the Prince and his aide seemed to know nothing of it, or else had chosen not to speak if they did). Scheherazade had felt safer not saying anything of what she knew. Such was the way of the caravan, that no-one had asked her directly what her business was. And now the caravan was gone.

After walking with firm steps, Sheherazade came to the promised ruined village just on dusk and slept that night in a broken temple, as Al-Haddar and the Prince's aide had insisted. She climbed on top of what was perhaps an altar as daylight faded and scuttling sounds came closer. The cries of unseen animals floated through the ruins. At dawn she searched for the well but could not find it.

She stumbled mid-morning into the shrine of Ersa with her feet blistered and the skin on her forehead peeling.

3

The House of Hakim and Zumurrad

'And so you have come here at last,' said the voice of the goddess. 'What a story. When did you leave Edessa? How long have you travelled?'

'About two days. I have today and perhaps tomorrow to find what I need, then I must return, because in four days my sister …'

'Marries Death the Destroyer …'

'Yes …'

'And who is it you said that you are looking for? The one who came this way looking for the cave of tales?'

'He is an old man,' said Scheherazade, 'his name is Ajedro …'

'Ah, the man with the monkey?'

'Yes!' cried Scheherazade. 'Do you know where he is?'

'He was carried into the village a week ago.'

'Carried?'

'He fell off his donkey while in the foothills and broke his leg, so I am told.'

'Oh, where can I find him? I must find him.'

'So, you didn't really come to the shrine for my sake?' said Ersa in a sly voice.

'This is the most beautiful shrine I have ever visited,' said Scheherazade. 'I think I will be your servant forever.'

'A good answer,' said Ersa. 'And I will forever be your mother. O, please don't cry again. It's just a thing that I say. Now, dear, go to the village. It lies under the black cliff that looks like a broken tooth. Hakim and Zumurrad have a guest house there. I believe the old man was taken there to recover.'

'Thank you, o goddess. I have a little silver,' said Scheherazade.

The little statue seemed to let out a sigh. 'Keep it. You will need it. *I* should pay you ... Leave something if you must. There is a well just behind the old temple-woman's house, there you can fill your waterbag.'

'Should I ask her?'

'No, I'll fix it up with her. You just go.'

Scheherazade heard again the soft scraping sound. She stood and put all of the silver pieces she had from Al-Haddar – seven 'eighths' in total – into a wooden box near the doorway and stepped out into the brightness of the day.

*

The path that ran from the shrine was a thin track in white mud. It joined an old road that bent towards black cliffs. Heat rose from the ground and burned her ankles. It was all so different from the forest. There, when you walked, you reached out and moved in a space wider than yourself, dappled with shadows; but in the openness of the desert, you became smaller. Every move had to be measured. And the vast uncertain spaces made Scheherazade feel sick. Was this the path? Were those the black cliffs? How was that one a broken tooth? How far should she walk before turning round and trying a different way? There were ten minutes of yawning blankness, but the black cliffs began to show habitations. Soon, a figure could be seen in motion, a woman with a few goats, and quickly it loomed up – a village nestling in and carved out of the cliffs.

In front of a looming wall of rock a small shaded market was quietly finishing for the day. It would be gone by the time the sun leaned over and scorched the ground. Blankets were piled with fruit and vegetables. A few patient vendors sat with near-empty baskets. Scheherazade had some small brass coins left and bought a handful of pistachios from a nut seller, thinking about Tonto and wanting to give him a treat. She heard a scuttling sound. Several monkeys had detached from the cliff face and ran over to her. The boldest began to jump up at her hand. Someone threw a stone and the monkeys went back to edging close. Scheherazade asked a fruit-seller – the stone thrower – about the guest house and they called over a young girl. The girl led Scheherazade to a house carved into the cliff face, where people milled around the entrance. The girl went in and a little while afterwards, a woman came out.

'Who is looking for the old man?'

'I am,' said Scheherazade. 'O, my mother, my name is ...'

'You have found the right house.'

The woman turned back inside and Scheherazade stood still, frozen to the spot by the roughness of the exchange. 'Well, come on,' said the woman's voice from inside.

The travellers at the entrance stared at Scheherazade. But after that, no-one seemed to pay her much attention. The inner courtyard was crowded. The woman, who she assumed was Zumurrad (it was), walked through the crowd, waving away questions and saying, 'Ask my husband!'

The rooms of the guest house were carved into the rock. Zumurrad brought Scheherazade to a small room with a curtain across the doorway. She pulled the fabric aside and led Scheherazade in.

Ajedro lay in a bed. It was hard to make him out from the wrinkled blanket that covered him. His eyes were half-closed, and his face was shrunken. He did not have his cap on. Scheherazade could see that death had made a first visit. She stood quietly for a moment, then spoke.

'O, my uncle,' said Scheherazade. 'It is I, Scheherazade.'

Confusion filled Ajedro's eyes and he tried to wet his lips. Scheherazade felt ill.

'He lay in the open for a day,' said Zumurrad, talking as if Ajedro was not in the room. 'They brought him out of the foothills. His leg was broken.' She went forward, lifted Ajedro's head and held a cup of water to his lips.

'What happened?' asked Scheherazade.

'We do not know, but he said that the monkey could confirm everything he said.' Zumurrad looked sideways at Scheherazade and tilted her head. 'He is very confused. His thoughts have become childish.' She lowered Ajedro's head to the pillow.

Ajedro stared at Scheherazade and something fell into place. The change that came over him was like that of a dry bush consumed by sudden fire. 'O, Scheherazade. My daughter ... Come here.'

He raised his arms and Scheherazade went and sat close to him.

'I was in the mountains,' he whispered, 'looking for ...' Ajedro's eyes saw Zumurrad and he turned his head to the wall.

'I will leave you together,' said Zumurrad.

She left the room and Ajedro relaxed. 'I found the Cave of the Five Golden Cups,' he whispered. 'Do you remember? I did not really hope to find it, but I did find it, O my daughter.' He rested, as if he had used up half his energy in speaking. After a few gasps for air he spoke again. 'As I came near, I saw in the shadows of the cave the glint and shimmer of gold. I went in, and there on a flat stone lay a golden book that seemed to sing. And by the book stood a golden cup. Could this be the book that holds all stories; and this the cup that gives to the one who drinks the power to speak them? I could not move! I was overcome! But not so the monkey! He ran forward, stuck his little head in the cup and drank from it. O, bad little monkey, I said. Tonto, bad monkey. But – marvel beyond marvels – he came back to me and spoke. He said in a little voice, "What has happened to me? I can talk." '

Ajedro laughed and coughed. 'I am out of strength. I must sleep, my daughter. Tomorrow you and I will go to the cave. There we will find treasures. I will show you. Your father will be very pleased.'

Ajedro lay back on the pillow and closed his eyes, drawing deep breaths.

Scheherazade leant in close. 'Where is the cave, o my uncle? I will have to go myself. I think you are not well enough to travel …'

But Ajedro lay still and said nothing more.

'O, my uncle, do not sleep. Tell me, where is the cave? How do I get there? I need to go now!'

Scheherazade felt a hand upon her shoulder. Zumurrad had come back in and gestured for her to leave the room.

4

To the Zagros Mountains

'Your uncle will sleep now until evening,' said Zumurrad. She led Scheherazade to the kitchen. 'He sleeps more often than not. You have been lucky to come when you did. You do understand that he will not leave here?'

Scheherazade nodded and tears burned her eyes.

Zumurrad asked her how she knew Ajedro. Scheherazade told her that he was a man from the neighbouring village, the owner of a bookshop. 'My father sent me to find him,' she said.

'You will have sad news to take back to him … and now *you* should rest. You are in my house and I insist. I don't need another invalid.'

'O, my aunt,' said Scheherazade. 'Can you tell me, where is the monkey?'

'Where is the monkey?' said a voice. There were footsteps, and a plump faced man entered the kitchen. Hakim, like his wife, was not big on introductions. He immediately threw some currants into his mouth and said, 'The monkey ran off and joined the other monkeys – there are some in the cliffs, near the market, also in the trees by the old cistern; but if you go looking, remember, that water is not for drinking. I've known some travellers who thought they could drink that water instead of paying the water seller. Well, they paid with a week of illness, and they had to pay me to stay here while they recovered. Water is not cheap ... nor is accommodation. The monkey. Yes, the monkey could be there. It could be anywhere.'

'I have seen it sometimes here on the roof of the stable,' said Zumurrad. 'The other monkeys I think did not welcome it.'

'Why does it stay away?' asked Scheherazade.

Hakim popped a nut in his mouth. 'After his fall the old man said the monkey could explain everything. And so I chased the monkey, saying, 'Come on, speak up!' I mean, who wouldn't? A talking monkey? Worth a fortune. But it ran away from me. And didn't say a thing. Mustn't have liked me. The old man kept saying the monkey would show us the way to the Cave of the Five Golden Cups, didn't he?'

'He did,' replied Zumurrad. 'He spoke of nothing else.'

'I need to go to that cave,' said Scheherazade in a voice louder than she meant. The thought that the cave was real, and that there was a book of tales – tales more powerful than Al'Adin or Sinbad – that could help Dunyazad ...

'Another mad one!' said Hakim with a grunting laugh.

Scheherazade could hardly keep still. 'Is there someone who can show me the way?'

'Oh, the way is easy,' said Hakim from under a raised eyebrow. 'You take the path that begins at the Fish Rock. It is only a mile from here. Then you ascend into the Zagros Mountains, avoiding, if you can, all the *djinn* lurking behind the rocks. And then you come to the foothills and there you find a thousand caves.'

'It is one of those?' asked Scheherazade.

'Yes. But there lies the problem. There are many caves – big caves, small caves, caves to keep a goat in, caves that house the dead, caves that are temples, caves that were temples – and so no-one is quite sure which is the actual Cave of the Five Golden Cups. If it ever existed in the first place!' Hakim slapped the tabletop and laughed. 'Though perhaps you could ask the monkey! Ha ha.'

'It is a story,' said Zumurrad pertly. She gave Hakim a look. 'My dear, take this food to the family in the Heracles Room.'

'But ... did he find the cave?' said Scheherazade trying to keep her temper.

'There is no such cave,' remarked Hakim. 'And if you go wandering in the hills, you end up wandering in your mind.' He tapped his finger against his head. Three slow taps.

Hakim exited the kitchen.

Zumurrad laid a hand on Scheherazade's sleeve. 'You are very tired. Come, rest. Search for the monkey in a little while. It is too hot outside now.'

Zumurrad took Scheherazade to a small room – a curtained alcove with a bed, where she could lay down. The space was just large enough for the bed, and there was a balcony, reached through two narrow louvred doors. Scheherazade cracked one of the doors open and looked out. The desert came right up to the roadway at the foot of the balcony. She craned her neck. The market square was empty. The village seemed abandoned. The heat rose in waves. She pulled the door closed, lay down, and fell into a deep sleep.

When she woke, it was night.

*

Scheherazade sat up in bed and began to breathe in a panic. 'Oh, Ersa,' she whispered.

Bars of moonlight lay on the floor. She wondered why they had let her sleep for so long.

She left the small room and moved on tiptoe over the stone floor. She heard a musical instrument, and a soft splashing sound, and followed the sound out onto a mezzanine. She shrank back from the moonlight. Below, in a courtyard, Zumurrad and Hakim sat by lamplight at a small table and drank tea. Zumurrad played a noisy game of solitaire, the cards going *ptep-ptep-ptep* as she slapped them down. An orange tree spread through half the courtyard. In front of Hakim lay a bag of coins and some papers.

'Enough to pay for everything,' he said, dropping a coin into the bag and spreading his hands. 'One week of accommodation, meals, watering and feeding the donkey, leaving nuts out for the monkey, five visits from the physician; one visit from the undertaker.'

'Is there enough there to pay for the girl to get home?' said Zumurrad.

'Doesn't she have her own money?' said Hakim. 'And why would her father send her by herself through the desert. Maybe he's half-baked, too.'

'I do not know. I think she will sleep till the morning. I will ask her then, after I break the news to her that the old man is gone.'

ptep-ptep-ptep went the playing cards.

Scheherazade fled back to her room and sat down on the bed, her hands pressed to her mouth. The strangeness of the place, the coldness and selfishness of Hakim, were the worst things she had ever known. Not even the death of her own mother had held so much fear. Then, there had been a small feeling that love still held them. Here, there was nothing. She listened and heard Hakim complaining about the cost of paprika, and about strangers passing through the village.

'They said that I must give them a list in the morning of all the guests ...' came the bored voice.

Scheherazade heard a scuttling sound. Something was out on the balcony. She quietly pushed one of the windows open. It was Tonto. It took her a moment to be sure, for he no longer wore his jacket or beret, and in the moonlight she could see that his ear had been torn in a fight.

'Oh, Tonto,' she said. 'Tonto! Come ... come.'

The monkey stayed still and looked at her.

'It's me, Scheherazade. I have something for you.'
She found the pistachios that she bought in the market
and held one out. 'Here!' she whispered. 'Book! Book on
shelf! Oh, please come in.'

Tonto looked at her blankly and did not take the nut.

'You know, don't you?' said Scheherazade. 'You know
that he is gone.' She spoke through tears. When she
looked up again, and wiped her eyes, the monkey was
gone. She pushed open the louvre and saw him now on
the edge of the balcony. 'Please don't run away. You
should stay with me now. I'll take you home … after …'

The monkey moved deliberately towards her and
looked into her eyes.

'After you find the cave?' said Tonto.

Scheherazade slipped backwards and landed on the
bones of her backside. 'O, goddess! You can, you can
talk!' she hissed. 'You can speak.'

'Shh! Not so loud!' said Tonto, scrambling towards
her. 'You'll bring the big man – that horrid big man –
and he said that if I could really speak then all their
fortunes were made. He said he'd put me in a cage and
show me off to the king. Was I going to say anything
after that, was I? "A talking monkey? Get him!" Don't
bring that man.'

'You can really speak. I will not call that man, I
promise. I hate him.'

'Did Papa tell you what happened in the cave?'

'Papa? … Yes. He did. Some things he told me. But
they said his mind was wandering.'

The monkey's shoulders sagged.

'We found a cave in the hills. In the shadows there was the light of gold. I ran forward while Papa led the donkey. I saw a golden cup on a stone ledge that seemed to whisper, and beside it was a golden book. I ran up to the cup and it had something in it, it looked sweet to drink, and I drank it. I went back to Papa and said, "What has happened to me?" For I could speak in your language. And Papa mounted the donkey in a fright and galloped away, but he fell. A goatherd found him and we were brought here. The big man scared me. So I went to live with the other monkeys. But ... O, I should find myself a quiet cave. I'll never be a tree-monkey like them. I've been too long with people of your kind. They laugh because I can't say their words properly. They call me all sorts of names and make fun. They say, "Look, it's a house monkey! Say something to us in *your* language!" or "Eek eek, what a nice little red cap and jacket." '

'Where *is* your little red cap and jacket?' said Scheherazade.

Tonto's mouth quivered. 'I will never wear them again!' he squeaked. 'And if you try to make me, then I am no longer your friend.' He folded his arms.

Scheherazade held all of the pistachios in her open hand. 'Here.'

The monkey took them and began to eat. He began to sniffle in the old way.

'Will you stay with me?' said Scheherazade. 'I won't chain you up. You can come with me. You'll be safe.'

'I might be safe,' he said in a small urgent voice, 'but you are not. You must come with me.'

'Why? Why must I? What do you mean?'

'Step out on the balcony. Look into the village.'

Scheherazade pushed the louvre and climbed through the opening.

The first thing she looked at was the sky. You could almost not see the darkness because the moon was so bright. The desert stretched away, silver and blue. It made her heart jump. She had no words to describe it, except that it was lonely, strange, and beautiful.

'No, look there.'

She looked down towards the market square, empty, except for some monkeys scavenging. As she watched, the monkeys ran off into the shadows. At the edge of the village, the way she had entered that morning from the shrine, she could see moving figures. Dark shapes turned into men leading black horses. She saw that they did not move like tired exiles.

'Who are they?' said Scheherazade.

'Soldiers. One rode up earlier and asked the watchman if he knew where Papa was. I heard this from one of the other monkeys, for they love to gossip. "Ooh, someone's looking for your master. Looks like someone's in big trouble."'

'Well … The soldiers burnt his house down,' said Scheherazade. 'I don't really know why. What has he done? Why do they want him?'

'They will not capture him now,' said the monkey. 'But it is still no good. The soldier asked after the young woman travelling with him.'

'What?' said Scheherazade in surprise. 'There was someone travelling with him? Who?'

'*You*! He is looking for you, nuthead.'

Scheherazade pulled back into the dark of the room. 'Looking for *me*. Why? What have I done?'

'He said that you were plotting with the rebels and are wanted by the king.'

'No!' said Scheherazade. 'It is wrong.' The feeling of being watched came over her.

'Right or wrong, he was waiting for some other soldiers to join him. And they have now come.'

Scheherazade looked at Tonto. 'I don't understand. I just want to get to the cave.'

'Why? You said just now that you'd take me home,' said Tonto.

'No. I have to find it.'

'What is so special about it?' said Tonto.

'I cannot save Dunyazad, or my father, without the book, without the cup. I can't stay here. I can't go back over the desert.'

Tonto put his hands on his head and squeezed his cheeks in thought.

'Come with me and I will lead you there. It will be safer there because there are many places to hide in the hills. They will not find you.'

Tonto jumped up onto the parapet of the balcony.

'But afterwards,' said the monkey, 'take me back with you to the forest. To the palace.'

'To the palace? To Edessa?'

'Yes.'

'Well, that's my plan. I must go back there,' said Scheherazade. 'Soon.'

'It is good then,' said Tonto. 'Now follow where I walk.'

Tonto dropped over the balcony to land on the level roof that was built out from the cliff. Scheherazade climbed down. She balanced with her hands stretched out. The cliff face, with balconies jutting out above her, was to her left. In looking up, her feet slid out from under her and she landed with a clash on the tiles.

'Shaishsheesh!' squeaked Tonto. 'What are you doing?'

Scheherazade's fingers clawed into the gaps in the tiles, but she slid only a short way. She crawled on her knees along the roof to where it ended above a small yard. She carefully and slowly made her way down the wall, but in the end slipped a short way down into the yard, landing on a pile of straw.

'Why are you taking so long?' said Tonto.

'Why are you making so much noise,' hissed Scheherazade.

'We must stay calm,' said Tonto, with his arms in the air. 'Here is where they keep the donkey.'

'Will we need the donkey?'

'Yes.'

'Why?'

'Just bring the donkey.'

Inside the stable Scheherazade felt around for a halter and found instead a rope that she slipped around the donkey's neck. She took a chaff bag, and took for herself a water bag that hung from a hook. There were some old cloths hanging up to dry and she tied these around the hooves of the beast. Dogs barked somewhere in the village as they slipped away. She filled the water bag in a hurry from a stone jar, but only filled it halfway before fear forced her to move on.

They took to a path and edged away from the cliffs into the moonlight.

Scheherazade looked back – her mind was full of the mysterious soldiers gathering in the empty marketplace, and what it meant that she was wanted by the king. Perhaps in running away she had brought danger on herself and Dunyazad.

She slid onto the back of the donkey and rode it along the gravel road, but keeping a little in the sand so that the steps were muffled.

'Hakim said that the path lies between two villages by Fish Rock.'

'He is right about that.'

'And it is really true that there is a cave of magical treasures?'

'Yes.'

'And a book of tales written on golden paper?'

'I saw it in the cave.'

'And a cup, that if you drink from it you receive the gift of storytelling?'

'Yes.'

'So, can you tell me a story?' said Scheherazade, wanting to know if it were as true as it seemed.

'What kind of a story?' said Tonto

'Well, anything. Surprise me.'

5

The Quiet Monkey

Once there was a baby monkey, with soft yellow fur, and beautiful eyes. He lay in his mother's arms in a tree in a forest where butterflies danced in shafts of sunlight. Forest deer nibbled at the leaves and crumbs of fruit cast off by the monkeys. The lizards did not have to wait long for an insect to fly by.

One day the little monkey began to venture away from his mother and went running up and down the outstretched arms of the tree. He ran to the very end, where the twigs meshed with the twigs of the neighbouring tree.

'Are you planning to jump onto the next tree?' said his mother. 'Well, if you are, you may go on to the next two trees, but once there, you must always come back to this tree before you set off again. Two trees and back – no more! I don't want you climbing onto a third tree. You won't miss out on anything by being careful, because most trees look the same anyway.'

And the little monkey did as his mother said, hopping from their home tree to the next, then the next; but always, after reaching the second, skipping back to where his mother sat waiting, peeling a fig, or picking little fleas off his sister.

But one day, something inside his monkey mind said, 'jump onto the third tree – go on', and he did. But another voice said, 'wait, you must always go back two trees worth', and this he did too, which brought him close to home, but not actually to his home. And when he saw his mother on her branch, peeling a green banana, something in his mind said, 'well, perhaps jumping onto the *fourth* tree is not so bad – it's not as if the fourth tree is any different from the third.' And so it went. And the little monkey began jumping on to the fourth, then the fifth, and the sixth tree. And it was then that the truth of his mother's words came to him. The trees did all look the same and he became lost. He skipped from tree to tree – back and forth – trying one tree, trying another. Even going up one very tall tree, but the white hot sky above the leaves gave no hint of where he should go. And the trees seemed to go on forever in all directions.

He overcame his shame at having disobeyed his mother and called out, 'Help me, help me! – it is I.' There was no answer. He called again, and this time he heard an answering call.

'Little one, come here, come here!'

The monkey was desperate to find his mother, and racing along branches he came at last to a tree that was different from the rest. It was hung with what looked to be vines. But they were not vines. They were the nets of a hunter, and they slithered closed around him, and the ropes drew tight. The hunter looked at the monkey, trussed up in the net and laughingly called out in a monkey voice, the sound that means 'little one, come here, come here'. The hunter laughed at the look on the little monkey's face and the little monkey bit his tongue and spoke no more.

From that day, the monkey was like a shadow. He was taken to a marketplace, and sat chained to a stool, next to bright-feathered birds in cages.

'Who would like to buy the saddest monkey in the forest?' said the hunter. 'Hardly a squeak! Doesn't even make faces. A very quiet monkey. Who would like to buy a quiet monkey?!'

'I need a quiet monkey,' said a woman. 'The parrot I kept screeched and squawked and learned bad words from the slaves, I had to get rid of it. I will buy the quiet monkey.'

And so the little monkey went to a house that overlooked a dark brown river, and he was chained to the perch once occupied by the parrot – fixed with the same chain. The little monkey remembered very little of his time in that house – except there was a little servant girl named Auri who handed out dates, but Auri died of a fever and was replaced by another servant who was not kind. The little monkey sat on his perch, day after day and needed no encouragement to stay quiet. He sat rocking, trembling – like a teardrop that will not fall.

The piece of black polished wood that was the monkey's perch was hardly the length of his body – not to be compared with the wide leafy branches of the forest. One night the little monkey woke and decided that life was over and he simply let go of the perch and fell. But the chain kept him hanging and swinging just above the marble floor. The chain cut into his leg, but he did not care.

The woman who had bought him in the marketplace came in the morning, saw the hanging body, and screamed with disgust. She called for her housekeeper, who unchained the monkey and walked with its limp body out on to the balcony that overlooked the brown river. The housekeeper tossed the monkey into the water.

But the little monkey did not sink, for it became tangled in some pieces of floating mangrove and drifted towards the sea, held up by mud and twigs. At the mouth of the river the water grew turbulent. It was salt water that now splashed the little monkey's face.

A ship from a foreign country was about to leave the river and sail north when one of the sailors looked over and saw the mess of floating twigs. A net sailed over the body of the little monkey and he was hauled quivering up onto the ship.

'We do be in need of a monkey,' said one sailor. 'Dos't think that it can be trained to fetch and carry?'

'First it needs water and a little biscuit,' replied the cabin boy. And so the little monkey began a long journey over the sea to northern lands.

But that little monkey never got his sea legs. The tall mast was nothing like the trees of his forest, it was a shaved stick with nets and ropes that ran up and down, and spars for the sailors. And he refused to climb it, for the nets reminded him of the nets that had taken him from his mother. Nor would he sit with the cabin boy as he mended the fishing nets, and so, huddled in a coil of rope, he became friendless.

One night the sea was calm – had been calm for five days – and the little monkey climbed down the side of the ship in the moonlight, carrying a piece of lead. He reached the surface of the still waves and pressed his face close to the water that was flat as a mirror. He stared more closely at the silver surface and there he saw a little monkey like himself looking back. He bent in closer. The monkey in the water came closer again. And the little monkey saw that there was someone else with him. It looked up and saw the eyes of the moon, looking at him with such sadness and yearning. And seeing that there was another one as sad as himself, if not sadder, he clung tightly to the side of the ship and did not let himself fall; but he let go his grip on the piece of lead, which vanished into the water with hardly a sound.

At the first port in the northern lands, the monkey was taken ashore. Once again to the marketplace.

'Who will buy this monkey?' said the cabin boy. 'It is a quiet monkey. T'will make a fine pet.'

'T'will make a fine purse,' called one.

'Five gold pieces,' said the cabin boy. 'For this rare monkey.'

'Five centimos if you're lucky!' said another.

The sun went down red over the sea, and no-one had bought the quiet monkey.

'Back to the ship, my lads!' said the captain.

'But what shall I do with the monkey?' said the cabin boy.

'You have your knife,' said the captain.

The cabin boy called out one last time, 'I'm giving this monkey away for nothing. Who will take it?'

'Time to go, lad,' said the captain.

So the cabin boy drew his knife.

A voice called out, 'I will take the quiet monkey.'

6

A Thousand and One Caves

Tonto fell silent.

'Where are we?' gasped Scheherazade, as if shaken from a dream.

'There. It is Fish Rock,' said Tonto.

A giant rock in shape like a gasping salmon leant out from the cliff. Scheherazade wondered if it had once been a fish, frozen by some magic of the mountains. The rocks and the moonlight were dazzling. Her mind was still in the story. She laughed without being able to help it. The monkey could speak and enthral his listeners. 'It is a magic drink indeed,' she whispered. 'Who took the little monkey?' she said to Tonto.

'I will tell you later.'

'Tell me now! Why did you stop?'

Tonto held up a finger for silence and pointed back along the way they had come. The whinnying of a horse half a mile distant came to them across the desert, distant but clear as a bell.

Scheherazade prodded the donkey. 'Oh, they are following. Is it this way?'

'Yes – this is the path. Kick the donkey!'

'What?'

'Kick the donkey. He's used to it.'

Scheherazade dug her heels into the flank of the donkey, but it kept up the same slow trot. Tonto jumped off and scampered forward. He raised himself up and called out. 'Move, you useless bag of bones! How much did I pay for you? A lemon! A lemon! The last of my hard-earned money for a nag! Ya, ya. So help me, I'll sell you at the next village and your new owner will turn you into glue! He'll turn you into six barrels of glue! Would you like that? Huh? Huh? Ya, ya.'

The donkey found new strength.

The path up the cliff was lined with dark bushes. They passed a group of people sleeping next to the path, who opened their eyes and watched without comment. Further on a man leapt up and held a stick, blocking their way.

'Get off that donkey. Now'

Tonto stood up on the donkey's head and let out a hiss like fingers scraping on a slate board. The man stepped back only a little and raised the stick higher. Tonto pointed two tiny fingers at his eyes, and then pointed these two fingers at the man. The stick fell from the man's hand and he fell back into the shadows, muttering in fright, saying words to fend off evil.

They moved on up the path, half-shadowed by the cliff, and at times the path went through ravines where the light all but vanished, but the donkey was sure-footed. Coming out higher, Scheherazade again looked back the way they had come. Nothing could be seen along the road, or out into the moonlit sand. She urged the donkey on, but Tonto did a better job, twisting its ear and insulting it.

After a while, the path levelled out and they found themselves on a plateau, with terraced gardens and farm buildings. But the houses were few and no-one appeared to stop them from moving through the little village. Scheherazade saw an oil lamp burning in a farmhouse window behind a square of hessian – the last of the dwellings – and after that the only light was from the moon and stars. The path melted into smaller tracks.

Ahead and rising up, like the shoulders of a lion, lay the hunched foothills of the Zagros Mountains.

'Oh, Ersa,' said Scheherazade. 'Al-Haddar the mule seller told me to keep away from this place.'

'He was right,' said Tonto, whose mood had become quiet.

Visible now, puncturing the slopes, were the first of several gaping holes – the start of the caves. As she looked, the hills revealed more and more of them, like black mouths. Her heart sank. As Hakim and Zumurrad had told her, the Cave of the Five Golden Cups could be one, or none, of the many she could see.

From far-off the whinny of a horse, followed by a chorus of dogs barking, drifted up the slopes.

'They are closer,' said Tonto.

'So, which cave is it?'

'It cannot be far,' said Tonto. 'The hills I remember were steeper – I think we go on, into that valley there.'

Scheherazade's heart sank, but she steered the donkey the way that Tonto indicated.

The first cave they came to was black against the blue-brown of the hillside. Scheherazade swung herself off the donkey and hurried over rocks to the opening. The ground was warm. She called out, 'Hello?' but her voice went back only a short way. This cave was nothing but a scratch in the hill. She picked her way over to the next dark entrance, but realised when she came to it that it was a compact bush with dark leaves. Not a cave. She ran back to the donkey, took the rope and moved on. At the next cave, moonlight fell through a shaft in the roof, revealing nothing but piles of broken stone and a rough shelter for goats.

She turned to look at Tonto, sitting perched on the donkey, his eyes darting nervously.

'Well?'

'Keep walking,' said the monkey.

The next cave was more promising. The entrance was high. Scheherazade called out, 'Hello!' and her voice echoed back. The cave was spacious and a place, at least, in which they could hide. She went a few steps forward, but Tonto jumped onto her and hissed, 'No! Do not step any further!' She stood still.

'What is it?'

'Step back!'

Tonto picked up a pebble and tossed it forward. They heard nothing, then *click-clack-click* all the way down, and finally *clunk*. The darkness swam around her and she stepped back into the bare night, quivering.

'We could have fallen!' she said.

'We must hide,' said Tonto.

'But not in there!' said Scheherazade.

'Then … find another cave.'

'They will find us and kill us.'

There was a cluster of caves fifty paces further up the hill and they made for this. But the donkey was now slowing them down. A sound of horseshoes clipping stones came drifting towards them. Scheherazade let go of the rope, abandoned the beast and ran. Tonto leapt from the donkey and followed her.

Behind them, down the slope, a light appeared. Scheherazade dropped into the grass and crouched low. The moonlight slowly revealed the soldiers and their horses. There were five of them, with one on horseback and the others leading their horses. One held a small lantern high on a pole.

Scheherazade stood and ran in a half-crouch up the hill. Tonto scampered alongside.

There came a whizz and something flew past, followed by laughter.

The cave that now presented itself had a wide but low entrance. Scheherazade ran straight towards the shelter of the opening. Her foot slipped on gravel. She landed on her face, but she was now in the mouth of the cave, scrambling into its shadow. A few twisted bushes grew around and over the entrance, with some hanging vines. She shrank down behind a boulder and gave up. She had no energy in her limbs. Tonto tucked himself in beside her.

'Run away,' said Scheherazade. 'They don't want you.'

She could see the soldier's faces now. Their eyes shone. They moved towards her. She could make out their clothing and their weapons in the moonlight. Swords, spear, crossbow, knives.

'Stand up and come out,' ordered one. 'Scheherazade, daughter of Jafar.'

A shadow fell upon the soldiers. They looked up and cried out in amazement and fear. Two fell to their knees in terror, fumbling for their weapons. One dropped the lantern. A horse reared up and clawed the air with its forelegs and the loose horses scattered.

Scheherazade looked up, but her view was cut off by the overhang of the cave. Directly above her the moon had disappeared and the sky was now black, as if a door in the air had swung open, showing darkness beyond. All she could do was lie flat, her face pressed against a stone. She could not even think. Tonto threw himself into her arms and trembled.

The mounted soldier drew back his arm to throw his spear, but from out of the blackness, an arrow whizzed down. The man fell from the horse. More arrows flicked down and struck the others. They cried as they fell. The arrows kept on pouring down until the only movement was from the horses.

The shadow drew back with a fluttering sound, and the moonlight flowed once more over the grass and the fallen soldiers.

But whatever was above her had not gone. Though Scheherazade could not clearly see it, or say what it was, what she had seen was a massive flying carpet, large and wide enough to carry the cloaked men who rode upon it. It seemed in size like a barge. This flying carpet circled around the donkey, which stood, nibbling a bush a short way back down the slope. The carpet came down to the level of the ground. As it turned, one of the men jumped off and ran up the hill, directly towards the cave.

'Scheherazade!' called the man. 'It is I, Ishaq.'

But Scheherazade had not waited. She had crawled into the cave as the moonlight shone out again, crawling on her belly under a low ceiling of rock, scraping her elbows. Tonto kept close. The floor of gravel and small stones shifted. She found herself sliding and tumbling down a slope, down some kind of chute, that spat her out after half a minute of falling and flailing into a vast chamber. She fell a short distance and her scream of shock as she hit sand gave the size of the place. The cave threw her cry of pain back at her until the echoes disappeared in a distant chamber.

She pressed her hands to her mouth. Her gasps for breath stretched out along a great distance. Tonto had clung to her all the way down. She could feel his small movements and clutched him to her.

She was lying on her back in a deep cave, but she could not really tell for the complete darkness. She heard a distant voice calling, and it sounded to her like Ishaq, but she pressed her hands over her ears, pressed herself into the stones, and closed her eyes.

Her first thought was to stay rigid as a tree. She was exhausted, and stunned by the fall. Reaching out for sleep she seized hold of it and hoped that she might never wake up.

Part 3

Ishaq and the Flying Carpet

*

ᚼᚼ In the days when Ali-Shar was emir, there was a deluge. For days the Great River was full of churning mud, debris, the wreckage of trees and houses, and animals riding by on floating logs. Three days later when the waters subsided, scavengers combed the riverbank. One man, Cacim, a disreputable dealer, discovered, half-buried in the mud, a sealed bottle. When he opened it, a *djinn*, in form like a boy, but beautiful as a girl, emerged and grew to the size of a small tree. 'At last!' cried Cacim, who had lost the family fortune through desperate and ill-advised schemes. 'At last – now I can have riches beyond the dreams of mortals!' The *djinn* bowed to him. 'Now, *djinn*!' cried greedy Cacim, 'I have freed you from your prison, grant me now my wish. I want to be richer than my no-good cousin Alem!' And in a moment, greedy Cacim was turned into a cloud of butterflies, for his rich cousin Alem had only the day before relinquished his immense wealth to become a holy man on the mountain, living a life of the spirit – knowledge that the *djinn* had, but of which greedy Cacim was unaware.

'Your wish is granted,' said the *djinn*, who then vanished away.

A witness to the dreadful event took the bottle, but no-one would buy it. Said one dealer in antiquaries,

'These bottles are such as are found in the Zagros Mountains, and they never brought anyone luck.'

from The Nights of Abu Nuwas

1

The Rebels

I have returned to this island in the estuary of Abodjan following the collapse of our hopes. My name is Gaspar son of Ahab, and I was a lieutenant under Ibn Al-Masudi. This is my testament.

Ibn Al-Masudi was sent in secret by King Zayn Al-Asnam to grow the rebellion against Tarquin the Destroyer, the white-skinned demon from the Northern lands. Because I had spent years going up and down the waters, and can easily ride a vessel through steep waves, I was chosen to help Al-Masudi, who sought, in particular, sailors and watermen to help him in his plans to remove Tarquin from his throne and overthrow Edessa.

Al-Masudi's schemes led us into the halls of blasphemy, and a price has been paid by those who least deserved it.

Al-Masudi ordered me to go and recruit men like myself, able-bodied, of medium build, easy in rough water. He also commanded that I should find people who worked in the citadel of the king, in order to learn the disposition of its rooms and corridors.

With these instructions I went upstream to the city of Edessa and plied the waters in front of the gates as a ferryman. From the villages along the way I recruited Al-Nadim, Jali'ad and Shimas (all now dead) – and a

young man from the forest near the city itself – Ishaq –
who I believe is also dead. This loss grieves me the most
for he looked on me as a father, and I could not save
him.

*

I found Ishaq walking by the river one evening and I
could tell from his manner that his thoughts had moved
in a direction perilous to him if discovered. I called to
him to step on board. He was surprised that I did not
charge him a coin. I said that I was happy to have the
company. Stepping in, I saw he had good balance. He
did not grip the gunwales as I moved the boat into the
most tumultuous part of the river. I tested him.

I spoke then to him about the resistance. I told him
what was written on his face, and that he should not act
rashly on his own, but with the rebellion. He was keen to
be guided. I found that Ishaq had been recently
employed in the treasure house of the citadel, caring for
a menagerie of exotic animals given to Tarquin as a
tribute. I urged Ishaq to keep at this work. This he did
and the court was pleased for him to bring into the New
Palace fabulous birds, small tamarinds, gentle gazelles,
and sometimes a panther, for the amusement of the
court. On my instruction Ishaq took opportunity to
become familiar with the layout of the rooms and
corridors.

I found from Ishaq that in the king's bedroom, behind a tapestry of a thousand eyes, there is a secret passage. It leads down to the peacock courtyard – a way of escape in the day of trouble; but also for us a means to infiltrate the palace. The discovery came about because Queen Amytis wished for some of the animals to be kept there, so she could look down upon them as they grazed in the courtyard; or go down by herself to sit quietly in that secret garden. Ishaq also found other defensive weaknesses, and these things I reported to Al-Masudi.

Al-Masudi, who was always the devious trickster under his mild and persuasive speech, received the news with disdain. He said I should direct my sight to the more obvious points of entry (I did not know at that time *how* he meant to get over the citadel walls). I should simply find out the number of sentries and their positions, said Al-Masudi.

Then an order came. With hardly any time to spare I was to bring myself and my recruits to a village in the foothills of the Zagros Mountains. Ishaq told his mother a story about wanting to find a refuge for his family in a neighbouring land. He could not tell her the truth. I could see that his heart was grieved. I then sailed down the Great River with Ishaq, we met up with Al-Nadim, Jali'ad and Shimas in the desert, and travelled on together under cover of night. We had begun our journey as the Terror of Tarquin began and knew that our mission could mean life and light to many; or death and desolation if we failed. But what was the mission?

I know little of the Zagros Mountains, or its legends. Having sailed on the deep for many years I was familiar with tales of sea serpents, fish-maidens, and magic islands, and was never convinced of their truth. But my young companions were excited to the point of frightening themselves as they talked of the legends of the Zagros Mountains.

I told them that our purpose was noble, and they should not act like a shoal of fish dreaming of a shark.

'But there are truly strange things in the mountains, o my uncle,' said Shimas one night. 'I hear that if you wander alone in the hills there is an evil wizard who leaps out on unsuspecting travellers and imprisons their souls in a bottle – you are turned into a *djinn* – and when released you are free to seek heaven on condition that you carry out a magic command of the one who breaks open the bottle.'

'And what command would that be?' I laughed. 'To cook the man breakfast?'

'Oh, no,' replied Shimas, 'the *djinn* must perform an act of dreadful magic.'

'But how does the *djinn* – if he only began as a poor traveller – acquire such magic?'

'I do not know, o my uncle, but I have heard that it is so.'

We travelled on for three days.

We came at last to our destination and entered the foothills at the Fish Rock. There we met more of our companions. We were a battalion of thirty – some

lieutenants like myself had recruited other young
warriors who were either skilled on water, or deft in
riding on animals. 'So, what *is* our mission?' asked Ali
Zaybac (a lieutenant like myself, and as much in the dark
as I was). Were we to attack in boats at night, riding
down the Great River? But that would only get us to the
walls and gates of the citadel. Or ride on wild stallions
and trample the gates?

We held our peace.

We were led to a cavern at the end of a ravine. The
stones of the entrance were carved, as if it had once been
a temple to a long-departed god; but the feeling that
came was that of a graveyard of unquiet spirits. My legs
became leaden as I walked towards the cave, fearing that,
too soon, all would be revealed.

2

The Trap

Al-Masudi was waiting for us inside the torchlit cave.
The first thing he did was to go round each man and
have them declare their name, and say where they were
from, what mattered to them most, and why they were
ready to die. Then he laid down the rules of secrecy and
obedience. 'We are here to fight for freedom, is that so?'
'Yes!' came our firm answers. And so with every
statement, and all of us responding 'yes', we were drawn
tighter into the tapestry he was weaving, pressing down
the threads of our obedience. Were we willing to do
what was needed? Yes. Were we ready to give of our
best? Yes. Was each man willing to give up his life for
his brother in arms?

Do I even need to write down the answer we gave?
You said it now in your own mind, as did we, falling
under Al-Masudi's spell.

Al-Masudi was accompanied by two alchemists.
When they spoke to him, he did not look at them. I
noticed that often he did not care to look any of us in the
eye, seemed not to think any of us worthy. It made us try
to please him the more. But he would also choose his
moments to drill his gaze into some one, or another. Not
many could bare that piercing stare of his, which I
believe he practised in a mirror.

The first alchemist produced a box and in it was a stone key. Al-Masudi took this mysterious key and walked to a wall of the cavern. Into a keyhole, which no-one had noticed before, he slipped the key, turned it, and the wall fell open, revealing a passageway. The walls of the cavern trembled in an eerie fashion.

I felt Ishaq grip my arm. He said in a small voice, 'O, my uncle, this is a dreadful place.'

Al-Masudi called out, 'Silence! We have started now, and there is no turning away. I need someone to go up this passage into the small cave that lies at the end. Our weapon lies there. A man can carry it out easily.' He spoke as if asking someone to fetch a coat he had forgotten to bring.

One young man snatched up a lamp and walked into the passageway. It was high-ceilinged, but narrow – wide enough only for two or three walking abreast. We saw the light recede. We craned forwards to look. The man walked with a hand outstretched to feel the wall beside him. Suddenly the light he carried went out. It fell into the floor and was gone. The man had vanished, without even a cry.

We shrank back, but Al-Masudi took up another lamp (on a long pole) and walked into the passageway. We followed slowly in the man's steps and found nothing but a dark shaft that filled the floor, too wide to jump over. Cold air swelled out of it.

'Bring the wooden planks,' said Al-Masudi.

The men rushed to bring planks – there was a pile of them waiting near the wall. Had Al-Masudi foreseen this trap? And yet not warned the man? Nothing seemed to disturb his calm.

The planks were laid over the gaping shaft. We could now walk over.

'I still need someone to go to the cave and fetch our weapon,' said Al-Masudi, examining a nail.

Then I knew that it was not just Al-Masudi's words, but some magic of the cave that was bubbling through the veins of the men, for Jali'ad stirred and stepped forward. I tried to grip his shirt and hold him back.

'I will go,' I said.

'No,' said Ishaq. 'I will go.'

What was this madness?

'Hail the watermen of the Great River!' said Al-Masudi.

But before any of us could step forward, another man, named Salim, picked up a lamp and strode across the planks. I think we three were stung by his bravery, and so I, Jali'ad and Ishaq hurried after him.

Thus we were able to witness closely what happened next.

'Do not walk so fast,' I called ahead to Salim. 'You do not know what is down here!' Salim was already ahead of us, and as if heeding my words, he slowed and stood still. But he did not stop because of *my* words; he stopped because a figure now stood in front of him.

Jali'ad cried out in fear. Because of the narrowness of the passage, and the gloominess, it was hard to see, and the lamp shone a little in our eyes. But as if from nowhere, a young woman was now barring Salim's way. Perhaps she had stepped out of a side passage, for a slight breeze was blowing, which twisted her robes and her veil moved like fabric in water.

She said to Salim, 'How *did* you get here?' – the words spoken in a way hard to describe; almost a kind of wonderment.

I heard Salim answer, almost in the same singsong tones, 'I rode on a horse.'

'A horse that never grows weary?'

'It rests. But I can sleep in the saddle.'

'But there is danger,' came the soft reply. 'What if ants come while you sleep,' she said, 'and eat the horse from the ground up?'

'Then I will reach up to an overhanging branch,' said Salim, 'and shelter in a tree. What then?'

'But I am the fire that consumes the tree,' said the young woman

'Then, I am the rain that quenches the fire.'

'But I am the cave that gathers the rain.'

'Then I am the bird that flies from the cave.'

'But I am the night that freezes the bird.'

'Then I am the bird that nests in the ground.'

'And I am the earth that covers you round.'

And with those words she was gone, and Salim fell over and did not move.

Jali'ad went forward and bent down to Salim. 'He is cold,' he said, his voice shaking.

Al-Masudi and the rest came up. The alchemists looked down amazed.

We reported what we had seen and Al-Masudi came close and pointed into my face and whispered. 'Afterwards, Gaspar, you will write down for me exactly what they said to each other.'

Some made to pick up Salim's body and take him out of the passageway, but Al-Masudi and the two alchemists said, 'No. No. We will be safer while he lies here. The spirit is appeased. Do not touch him.'

Ishaq took up Salim's lantern and walked forward without a moment of hesitation. Jali'ad and I followed.

'We will never leave here,' said Jali'ad.

I had taken a lantern on a pole and moved quickly ahead of them. Having recruited these little-more-than-lads, I could not leave them to walk in front of me to their death.

3

Into the Pit

'Look for anything that might open or close, slip, or slide,' I said. 'Any rock that might fall, or gap in the wall from which arrows might fly, or a crack in the floor ...'

'Steps,' said Ishaq. 'There, I see steps.'

Before us in the passageway were some steps, hard to see, and powdered smooth by years of falling dust. The steps went down into a trough that continued under an overhang of the cave roof, just visible in the lantern light, with matching steps ascending on the other side.

'This was once a pool,' said Jali'ad. 'There are marks of water on the walls – do you see?'

'It has been dry for a long time,' said Ishaq.

'Perhaps this trench was filled with water, right up to the step here,' I said, 'and not seeing the dark water ahead, you fall forwards, into the pool.'

'And so drown?' said Jali'ad.

'Drowning is the least of our worries,' I said, and stepped forward. But Ishaq held me back.

Ishaq carried a spear. He began now to tap down on each of the steps, to see if anything rocked or moved. Nothing stirred, nothing changed, nothing flew out or flew down.

'But if this was meant to only make you fall in, why are there steps down, and up through there, beyond?' said Jali'ad.

'It is a defence,' said Ishaq, 'filled with water it keeps out intruders, but it will be emptied, should you, the master, want to go in yourself.'

'So, if this pool is empty, then that means someone is at home?' said Jali'ad.

'If the master is home, then it is no man,' I said.

Ishaq was now at the bottom of the step. The trench levelled out into flat sand. Ishaq put his foot forward and there came a sound like the crunching of an eggshell. He withdrew his foot and retreated back up the steps. Then, with the spear, he leant over and probed the sand. He fished from it the skeleton of something like a snake with its head crushed. He moved the spear around to lift out more skeletons of sharp-toothed serpents that filled the trough to a depth of a man's knees.

'It is an ancient trap, then,' said Jali'ad. 'You fall in the water and are consumed by serpents.'

'Once, in days gone by,' said Ishaq. 'But there is no-one here now. I feel sorry for these creatures as the water dried up.'

'They would not feel sorry for you!' said Jali'ad with a bright laugh.

'Be calm,' I said. 'We are not through it yet.'

Al-Masudi was now behind us. 'Clear a path,' he ordered with a triumphant note. 'The danger is past. The water here has been gone for ages.' He gestured for us to come up from the steps. Three men now jumped in and began to spade a way through the twisting mess of bones and sand. Al-Masudi turned and went back to the main cavern.

But, of course, this place was not dead. The apparition that killed Salim was proof of this. I heard the first man shovelling the bones to one side. His spade reached down to the floor of the dry pool, scraped on stone, and perhaps it struck something. A latch? A lever? Who can say. But suddenly all the bones were moving. I saw in that dry pit of bones the shapes of serpents with gaping white jaws. They moved, they writhed, and took on living forms. The three men in the pit cried out and were gone.

One of Al-Masudi's alchemists staggered forward onto the steps as the rest of us shrank away in horror. He was holding a small amphora and poured the contents out. A heavy, bluish smoke dripped onto the steps and spread over the base of the pool. The alchemist jumped away and signalled for the rest of us to pull back. He covered his mouth with a cloth.

There was an evil smell – of drains, of burnt hair. And the bones became still.

Said the man: 'Let it settle … We have not long before they come to life again. Go now if you will. And take as few breaths of the vapour as you can.'

Ishaq jumped down and waded through the blue smoke and the bones.

He ducked down as he reached the overhang and was through to the other side. We saw him ascend the steps. And we waited. It was only the space of a minute. He reappeared and came back down the steps into the trough once more. He was carrying something that looked like a log, with bands of cloth around it. It could have been a large scroll. It was clearly not heavy, not solid as a log, but he carried it carefully. But Ishaq stumbled and fell back on the steps and I knew that it wasn't a matter of balance. He was sick. His face was flushed, his eyes rolled up as if he would faint.

'This potion of yours!' I cried to the alchemist. 'What is it?'

'Make him run back,' was the man's answer. 'He has not long. Tell him not to breathe in the fumes.'

We held up the lamps and I could see Ishaq's face turned our way. I shouted to him, told him to stand and walk, to follow my voice, and he heard me and staggered forward. He was now back amongst the bones and walking towards us, holding the prize.

The alchemist had said we did not have long, and the villain spoke the truth. A shiver went through the bones. We could see the flick of a bony tail, a ripple of a serpent's ribcage, a skull that seemed to gasp for breath, snapping jaws with needle-sharp teeth.

And we were all calling, shouting, 'Here, here. Ishaq. Come this way. This way!'

Ishaq was now through the overhang and wading slowly through the bones and the blue poison. His legs sank down as if it was quicksand? But the bluish smoke was fading and his eyes came clear with a growing awareness and terror. He knew that the serpents were starting to wake. He was now halfway to us, now three quarters of the way. His face was ashen. He was almost with us, but stopped walking, threw up and fell forward on the stirring sand.

Jali'ad jumped in to save him and stomped through the bones, which seemed to whip around him like tentacles of an octopus. Jali'ad reached Ishaq. I stepped off and felt as if I had plunged into water filled with rough-skinned eels. Something jabbed at my leg and later I found an angry welt and teeth marks on the skin. I went forward, but Jali'ad already had a grip on Ishaq, and so I jumped back up the step. Helping hands pulled me free, but my head began to swim. I lost all strength and sat down.

Jali'ad with Ishaq came to the foot of the steps. Arms reached down and pulled Ishaq up, along with the prize. But it was too late for Jali'ad. In his last moment, joy was on his face as Ishaq was lifted to safety. 'Well done,' I croaked. But as Jali'ad mounted the steps, something leapt up and he was snatched away into the darkness of the pool. The sands covered him.

The alchemist, wailing and cursing, was there to throw another amphora of his poison into the pool, but it was of no use now. We watched the blue smoke spread again and the boiling sea of bones stilled itself. We fled.

The men lifted and carried Ishaq out of the passageway, past the body of Salim, and across the planks that covered the pit, and out into the cavern. Ishaq looked dead. The alchemist and his aides poured water over him. They made him drink physick (they poured it down his throat) and they bade us – we who had been on the steps – to wipe ourselves down with the same stuff, and also to drink. The medicine smelt and tasted foul.

Some of the men vomited. My insides wrenched. I fainted, and felt myself falling down a deep shaft, even though the ground was cold and still beneath me.

4

Al–Masudi's Secret Weapon

When I woke, it was Ishaq who was shaking my shoulders. I must have looked more dead than I felt, because tears sprang to his eyes when I opened mine to look at him.

'You are alive,' he said.

'Yes,' I replied. 'And you, too. Forgive me, my son. Where are we?'

'Back in the cavern, o my uncle. Please tell me, can you move?'

'I can,' I said, trying my limbs and finding that I spoke the truth, even though they moved stiff as brine-soaked rope.

'Come to this side of the line,' said Ishaq.

'What line?' I asked. There was a quietness all around. I turned my head and saw that there was a line scraped in the sand of the cavern floor. It ran between Ishaq and myself.

'I am on this side of the line. Come over to me,' said Ishaq. 'Come over to this side of the line.' I looked around. All the members of the battalion were gathered in a group, looking in my direction. I wondered why I was on the other side of this line.

I turned my head and there laid next to me was the body of Salim. I rolled myself over towards Ishaq and he lifted me up. It turned out that Al-Masudi had drawn the line to separate the dead and the weak from the living and the courageous. I had missed out on hearing this particular speech (Ishaq told me the details later).

I was glad that I had been senseless while Al-Masudi poured out his bilge.

Al-Masudi now called on the alchemist, who cut the bands around the tube that Ishaq had recovered. I could see now that, rolled out, the thing was a carpet. The weave was simple and elegant. There were lines and markings that resembled script. There were small purple tassels along all sides. We gathered round to look at it.

'Some *one* to sit or stand on the carpet,' said Al-Masudi generally.

One man stepped forward and put his foot on the carpet. And straightaway he was thrown through the air, as if an invisible hand had seized him and tossed him sideways. I do not think his foot even touched down upon the threads. We were amazed.

'Try again,' said Al-Masudi, 'but crawl on, slowly.' The warrior picked himself up. He lowered himself onto all fours, looking as if he would punch anyone who laughed at him, and slid like a crab onto the carpet. He was thrown off again and landed sprawling. The man stood up with his fists clenched.

Then Al-Masudi himself stepped forward and spread his hands. He said a single word – said it softly, so that we could not hear it well – and stepped on to the carpet. He was not thrown. Now came the moment of greatest challenge for him and he passed the test. He said to the carpet, 'Rise', and it floated off the ground. The men drew back. I could see in Al-Masudi's face the slight quiver of a man desperate to keep his balance and not wishing anyone to see it; but the moment passed. He stood, legs slightly bent, and did not topple over. He spread his arms wide and said something else to the carpet and it moved around the men in a wide circle, moved even over the body of Salim. Al-Masudi returned triumphantly to where he began.

But he did not stop there. He sat down on the carpet, like the master of a house, or a king upon his divan. And hovered in the air before us. Suddenly the carpet flashed away and completed another circle, this time faster, and this time making the men dive to avoid being struck on their heads. Al-Masudi was smiling and laughing. And now the carpet shot away out of the cave and we were all left standing. Some ran after Al-Masudi, out into the open. But Al-Masudi glided back in, and the men began to cheer, and clap their hands. He raised his arms in the air and laughed.

'To the ground,' he said. And the carpet lowered itself once again to the floor of the cave.

He immediately stood up and found a rock to perch on.

'Now you have seen the start of our plans. Here is a magic carpet. And what can it do? It can carry a man. It will carry any of you, who ride rough water and wild beasts, with ease. How far can it go? I believe the distance is endless. You could ride on this to the pillars of the world, and see the great cataract falling off into the night. In an instant you could fly to the highest mountain and freeze your beards – most of you! – and return to the warmth of the desert with the icicles still hanging. Speed, and distance. This is faster and stronger than ten war horses, swifter than a boat with eight oarsmen. And it will carry you over the walls of the citadel at Edessa!'

We gasped our approval, cheered.

'On this you can fly into King Tarquin's bedchamber and be the one to free the world of the white-skinned demon!'

A great speech, but parts of it were dangerous. Yes, the carpet could take you to a mountaintop in an instant, but woe-betide the passenger who made that wish. One man tried to fly to the peak of a mountain in the blink of an eye – he was simply blown off and fell to his death on the rocks. A man was sent to climb and fetch the carpet back. When he rode it back he rode it slowly.

But I am getting ahead.

Al-Masudi had said 'a man could fly into the king's bedchamber' and our eyes lit up at the promise of such a quick victory. I felt Ishaq standing tall. He had even stepped forward.

'So, one man?' said Al-Masudi. He turned to me. 'What do you say, Gaspar, son of Ahab?'

5

The Magic of Ibn Al-Masudi

My head was still swimming, but as a soldier sworn to serve, I had to answer my leader. 'I think there is a good chance,' I replied.

'A good chance? Tell us what you know? How will it work?'

'Ishaq has worked in the Palace in Edessa, even in the Royal Chambers. He knows the rooms and the corridors. We have drawn up a diagram.' I took from the inside of my coat some papers and presented them. 'And further, he has discovered a secret passageway, from a small courtyard garden into the king's sleeping chamber.'

'And so,' said Al-Masudi, 'Ishaq – who we all agree is one of our bravest – could fly over the walls of the citadel, come to rest in the courtyard, and then infiltrate the room by this secret passage?'

I was feeling light-headed and sick, but I replied, 'Yes.'

'And the guards positioned on the walls of the citadel would not see him fly in?'

'He would go in by night.'

'And how would he know where to go – would he carry a lantern?'

'Perhaps,' I said.

'And perhaps be seen and plucked from the sky by an arrow?'

'He would follow the lights inside the palace, then.'

'Brave King Tarquin sleeps with the light on?'

'I do not know,' I replied over the mild laughter.

'Will the king cry out when struck by our swift assassin? Will he die immediately?'

'I do not know.'

'It is no matter to me if he squeals like a pig – but then, there will be guards in the room in an instant. And Ishaq – if indeed he is the one who rides the carpet – will be taken. Is that a small possibility?'

'It is,' I admitted.

'And then questioned. You know what I mean by questioned?

'I do.'

'Not something that Ishaq's family would wish to know about, that is, if his family were even allowed to live. You see, you say there is a "good chance" of a single man gaining entry, but the risk is too great of having that one man captured and then revealing that his commander is Ibn Al-Masudi, who works on behalf of King Zayn Al-Asnam. And that is a truth that can never be revealed.'

Al Masudi, while I answered him, kept his head turned away. Now he turned and looked at me sorrowfully. 'We need more than a "good chance".'

'I will do what your wisdom suggests,' I said.

'Wisdom suggests,' said Al-Masudi, 'that we send in a small but potent force. Not one brave man – and I know you are all brave men. We send in a force that is like to the crew of a fighting ship – some armed with bows and arrows to 'pluck from the board' the sentries; some skilled in ground fighting to 'remove the knights', some to watch, some to act. A force that will not only kill the king, but hold the high ground, with no need to retreat. An unbeatable force.'

'But …' It was my comrade Ali Zaybac who spoke up. 'But how will we all fit on to the one carpet?'

There was some laughter, which was cut short by Al-Masudi's voice, declaring: 'We fit on it like this!'

He ordered two men to pick up the carpet and grip it tight. They held it at either edge. As they did so, Al-Masudi took from the box, the one that had held the stone key, a long knife with a twisted blade.

'Not *one* carpet,' he cried.

With that he seized the carpet at its edge and dragged the knife through it from top to bottom, slicing it in two.

I flinched, and think that others did as well. The two men who held the carpet staggered apart – their faces filled with terror. One fell and cried out, more scared than pained, but each man still held his piece of carpet. The other man dropped his and stared at his hands as if stung by a jellyfish, but he quickly snatched the carpet up again.

And then he cried out, as we all did, when we saw what he held: his piece of the carpet was the same size as before. The carpet was unchanged. And when the other man scrambled to his feet, he also held a carpet the same as the one that the other man held. Neither carpet was less than the other.

I can swear they were the same carpet, with the same simple pattern and decoration. The purple tassels ran all the way round the border. The carpet was not damaged from having a knife go through it. Except that it had become two.

'And thus we make a transport for all of our men,' said Al-Masudi.

I became aware of a trembling in the stone floor beneath my feet.

But Al-Masudi was now intent on his work. Having spoken he again sliced through one of the carpets – and it became two. And again and again. No-one could see how it 'worked'. He cut with the knife until there were thirty carpets on the floor of the cave.

I said 'not damaged', but there was damage. I felt as if I had been cut in two. I felt as if together we had hurt something innocent. Shimas came up to me and said quietly, 'It is dangerous.'

'We cannot go back now,' I said in a haggard voice. 'Our only hope is to do exactly what he commands. And maybe someone will forgive us.' There was a humming in my ears. I felt unsteady on my feet.

Ishaq stared at the ground. 'It is an earthquake ...'

The ceiling of the cave cracked. Small stones and shards fell on us.

'Each one take a carpet,' cried Al-Masudi. 'We must leave this cave now!'

We scrambled like crabs to pick up the carpets and made for the opening of the cave. Already small pieces of rock and dust were dropping on us. I stood trembling like a lamb, my limbs still fevered and weak. Ishaq and Shimas grabbed hold of my arms and led me out of the cave. As he did, a slab of stone came away from the ceiling. We were blown into the open in a mighty gust of air and billowing sand. When we had recovered – and the ground still sang like a gong – we saw that others had joined the dead men in the cave – never to come out again. This included one of the alchemists and his helpers, and other warriors, including our own Al-Nadim. We called for him. We called and called, but he did not come.

Shimas put his arms around me and Ishaq, and the two young men wept. I was too ashamed to weep. What had I brought them to?

But Al-Masudi went round counting his men and counting the number of carpets. I think that five carpets were left in the cave. With little expression on his face Al-Masudi began again to cut with the twisted knife, and clouds thickened in the sky.

We stood outside the cave. Dawn was a way off and we had only a few flaming torches to watch Al-Masudi continue his work, like one who had no need of sleep. A cold wind began to cut in. The torches blew out and rain drove down upon us so that we stood shivering.

Shimas found Ishaq and I some blankets – we were both still unwell from the exposure to the poison.

Shimas went to find us food. A good man in any situation, he found a safe shelter – a small cave that looked secure – and was able to light a fire and heat water.

I sat under my blanket by the wall of the new cave and thought back to why Al-Masudi had spurned what we had discovered about the secret passageways in the palace. A trained fighter *could* go in and kill the king, and then escape. One magic carpet would have been more than sufficient. But no, Al-Masudi shaped his arguments so that there seemed to be no other way but to cut the carpet into parts. An act of irreverence that doomed us all.

6

The Riders

Over the following days the trembling in the ground subsided and the air grew warm. The skies were clear. This provided some comfort, as it must always do; but fear like a bird perched on my heart.

Al-Masudi taught us the words required so that we could ride the carpet. One must speak the word *sirocco* in an open manner – only then will the carpet allow you to sit or stand or ride on it.

The first time I did it, I prefaced the word *sirocco* with a statement of sorrow, a plea for forgiveness.

Al-Masudi caught me at it – praying to the carpet.

'Ha,' he said for the benefit of everyone, 'You old sailors, you are so superstitious.' He clapped me on the shoulder. 'It works, you know, just as well with or without prayers. Everybody listen! Your skill in staying balanced is what will save you. Courage, to do what is needed, is what will bring us victory.'

We all found the carpets easy to ride – as I said, we were skilled watermen, or riders of animals. But I felt that the carpets were being easy on us, perhaps too compliant. I have mentioned the warrior who requested to go to the mountaintop in a moment and was killed. Though the carpets were easy for us to ride, everyone, after that man's death, minded their manners.

Al-Masudi was mostly pleased with our progress. But a carpet – as Al-Masudi had observed – while it could easily carry a single person, could only perform in a limited way. A second man could ride upon the same carpet (say a man with a bow and arrows), while the first man attended to manoeuvring; but the carpet would bend and 'roll' unevenly with two on board attempting anything other than flight in a straight line. So Al-Masudi ordered four carpets to be lashed together by knotting the tassels. Four became 'one'. Al-Masudi found that this freed up men to give their minds to fighting. The larger carpet then became like the raised fighting top of a warship.

It was a small step from there to lashing all the carpets together. The now enlarged carpet flew with the expected constraints of a large, weighty 'vessel'. It could not move nimbly, and it could only turn slowly, or else ripples and waves shivered across the 'deck'. Once, the whole thing folded in on itself from the weighty centre and plummeted. We lost two men in that incident – one killed, and one badly injured who did not last through the night. Al-Masudi lashed some poles across the carpet to dampen these tremors.

I saw that the carpet always moved uneasily, bending like a beast that groans to be freed, beating the air in slow strokes like a great ray beats the water, or as an elephant sways from side to side before it charges.

I instructed Ishaq and Shimas quietly to pray to the carpet, to show reverence and pity for the plight it was in, to express sorrow in their hearts.

But despite our fears, Al-Masudi's plans proceeded, apparently well. He now had the greatest weapon the world had seen: a flying ship with a warrior force aboard. He marked whitewash upon the sides of a cliff and told us that the first mark represented the walls of the Caliph's palace in Samarkand, another the height of the walls of Constantinople, the last, the walls of the citadel in Edessa. We coasted up and over the 'walls' of Edessa with ease.

Next, we were supplied with dark robes to hide our progress during the night and learned skills, such as firing arrows from the moving carpet, or jumping and rolling from the carpet while it glanced over the ground. And perhaps we would succeed after all. My plans of the palace proved to be useful. Al-Masudi had us carry out practice runs over low stone walls that represented the citadel, down to a place marked out as the Pavement of Judgement (the portico outside the king's residence). We were able to clear the mock wall, bring down the mock sentinels and guards.

One night there came word that, despite our travelling in secret, and the unquestionable loyalty of all the men, soldiers of King Tarquin were reported making their way up the Fish Rock into the foothills. Al-Masudi ordered us to attack them.

The night this happened was quiet, the moon was almost at the full coming up to the Night of Nights. Once the scuffling of shoes on the rocks and stones had stopped, and all the warriors were standing on the carpet, the feeling was of standing on a ship about to slip away with muffled oars onto a dark ocean. We rose into the moonlit sky, came down the valley and over a ridge to see below us a small party of soldiers. One carried a lantern. They were spread out as if searching for something. Someone said that they saw a young woman fleeing from them. The archers went forward while some of us went to the stern to give balance. The archers fired and brought down the handful of men.

But then, one of our men leapt from the carpet while it was near the ground and raced in the direction of a cave. I did not realise, until it became clear that he had disappeared, that it was Ishaq. I could not fathom what he was doing.

Ali Zaybac came to me angrily. 'Ishaq has run away?! I gave no command! Did you tell him to do this?'

I could not believe it. 'No,' I said. 'He must have seen more of the enemy and he has run to engage.'

'The young fool. Where is he? He has been taken,' was his reply. 'We have been discovered.'

Ali Zaybac ordered some of the men to be ready to charge the caves. But the carpet was turning away and rising, as if caught in a sudden swell. The men who controlled the four corners were bidding the carpet to stay and come back down to the ground. It disobeyed. I was reminded of the sailors in the story who camped on an island, only to have it revealed that the island was a monster, which overturned and drowned them all. We were now rising dangerously high on our 'island' in a sea of air.

With no warning, the knots that held the carpets together came loose along one meridian, and a whole section trailed in the sky. Unfortunate the men on that side! Four or five fell off into the dark of the night and were thrown down into the valley. I saw Shimas fall. Everyone else clung on in fear – crying whatever prayers they had to their gods – and waited for death.

One of the 'steersmen' was able to persuade the carpet to fly back to our encampment. Perhaps the carpet had shown enough of its anger; or else it wished to show Al-Masudi who was the true master.

At our camp Al-Masudi was angry and wanted a reckoning of our failures. Ali Zaybac told him that, despite the loss of our men, all of Tarquin's soldiers had been disposed of, but that Ishaq had leapt off and disappeared, and in that confusion, we had lost control of the carpet.

Al-Masudi said through gritted teeth, 'I did not expect him to be such a coward, or perhaps it was clear from the start. A spaniel keen to please its master, but at heart a cur.'

'He is not!' I shouted. All of my young recruits were now gone. 'It is your madness that has brought us here.

And now this thing you have made is taking revenge on us all.'

He looked at me as if I was a donkey blocking the road. He turned to the men, who had heard. 'And does anyone else believe this old washerwoman?'

Al-Masudi walked over to his tent and threw open a chest that was standing near the entrance. In it were some bottles made of black glass.

'You are a big disappointment, Gaspar,' said Al-Masudi. 'I should have left you on the broken-down boat you call home, fishing for mud crabs.'

He took one of the bottles and threw it at the ground. There was a shifting of the moonlight and what looked like the ghost of a man formed in the air before us, as large as five men it seemed. I remembered Shimas' words about imprisoned spirits – that this *djinn* must perform some act of dreadful magic – but I was now no longer surprised by anything that was happening.

'My wish,' said Al-Masudi, addressing the spirit, 'is that you take Gaspar son of Ahab back to where he belongs. Then have your freedom.'

As if in some dreadful dream the spirit surged upon me, around me, inside me – I felt as if I breathed it in. The world was spinning and tumbling and I found myself plunged in water. The thickness of the spirit left me. Again, as if in a dream, I saw a man with a look of rapture on his face running away with his hands raised. My hands found a rope in the water. I seized hold of it and followed it. It was the rope that tied my boat to the jetty in the estuary of Abodjan. I pulled myself, gasping for air, out of the salt water and up onto the planks of my boat.

*

I do not know what happened after these events. Perhaps I will hear the news soon that Tarquin is dead and replaced now by the Great Ibn Al-Masudi. Victorious at last, but at what price?

Part 4

The Beast King

*

ᴄꙅ A merchant was riding his mule into the desert,
leading nine other pack mules, when a young boy came
out of the shelter of a cave and approached him. The boy
asked the merchant if he would let him ride one of the
animals, for the path now diverged from the hills, the
mild days of Spring were at an end, and it was a full day
in the open sun to the oasis of Al-Borodin. 'Surely,' said
the merchant, who was a kind man. As they rode along,
the merchant asked the boy from whence he came, and
asked the name of the boy's father and mother. The boy
spoke of his home in a village in the hills behind them,
and of its famous well where holy men came to pray.
Suddenly a storm drew its fingers across the expanse of
desert. The sands billowed and the merchant had to
hurriedly tie cloths around the eyes of his mules – the
boy helping him in this task. They rested as the storm
blew across them, and then rode on, though the
lingering dust made it hard to see. The storm faded as
they came to the oasis of Al-Borodin. On dismounting,
the merchant found that the boy had vanished.
Troubled, he ran to find the headman of the oasis and
asked that a search party be formed to go and find the
lad.

'Ah,' said the headman, 'over the years, many
travellers have given a ride to the same boy. It is said he

had a secret that was too terrible for his family to bear, and he planned to leave his village and cross the desert to Samarkand, but the parents gave the boy to the uncle, who killed him and threw his body in a well. He never left his village.'

'What is the name of that village?' said the merchant.

'Oh,' said the headman, 'I do not know. But it is one of many in the Zagros Mountains.'

from The Nights of Abu Nuwas

1

Scheherazade and the Golden Cup

Scheherazade, after she woke, lay still for a long time with her eyes shut tight. She did not want to open them, knowing what was to be seen – a tomblike darkness. But when she did open her eyes, because there was nothing else to do in the cave, she saw, in the darkness, a golden light. It was a pale autumn colour. The fear drained away like water from a broken jar.

'Tonto?' said Scheherazade. 'Are you there? Do you see that light … there! It is morning. It is a way out of here! Tonto?'

There was no answer. 'Tonto, are you there? Please, please be there. Where are you? There is light coming into the cave.'

'I am here,' came a croaky answer, followed by a few monkey coughs. She could see the light reflecting now in Tonto's sad eyes.

'I can see daylight.'

'No, you can't. It is not daylight.'

'What is it, then?' asked Scheherazade. She crawled forward over pebbles and rock to look closer, but moving a short distance did not bring it nearer.

'It is the golden light that I saw in the Cave of the Five Golden Cups.'

'The cup? We have found the cup!? Oh, Tonto, stay close.'

'I cannot move easily. My leg was hurt in the fall.'

Scheherazade crawled back and reached around in the dark, frightened when she could not find him, and her hand felt for his little face.

'I'm such a hopeless monkey. Will you come back for me?'

'I'm not leaving you! Climb on me, hold on tight – we'll go together. I'd lose you in the dark if I left you here, and I don't want to go on alone.'

Scheherazade raised herself on to her knees and Tonto climbed slowly onto her back. Half of him was a dead weight, but he was warm around her neck. She began to carefully crawl forward.

'Why are we here again?' he said.

She told him about the king, and how Dunyazad was on a list to marry him, how even the best storytellers – even Amirah, daughter of Massoud – were being slain, and how the only sure way of saving Dunyazad was to find a magical, enchanting story. Something extraordinary that she could use to save herself.

Tonto let out a short sniff. 'Strange. You don't even like each other.'

'What?' gasped Scheherazade. 'What do you mean?'

'Whenever I have seen you, you always look on her as if you're chewing on a clove. You're always squabbling about something.'

Scheherazade lay down in the darkness and cried. 'She is young,' said Scheherazade. 'And she is annoying.

And we have no mother. And she never does what I say. I might as well talk to the oven.'

Tonto leant over and stroked her cheek.

'I never really knew my sister,' he said, 'so do not know if we would have fought or been gentle with each other.'

'If I have to,' said Scheherazade, 'I will drink from the cup. And marry the king. And tell him a story …'

'Don't do anything foolish,' said Tonto. 'You are *my* only hope.'

Scheherazade sat up and began to crawl forward, though her side ached from the fall. Slowly she began to cover the distance and came eventually to a narrow passage that sloped upwards.

Over the minutes the blur of gold began to shape into a square of dim light. Scheherazade hoped that it would turn into something they could walk through. But then the end of the passage was in front of them, a dead-end wall, and the light turned out to be from an adjacent cave, coming through a hole that not even the monkey could climb through. Scheherazade bent a little and peered through the opening. The hole, rectangular in shape, was just wide enough to let her hand through. And she could see that the light came from a golden book and a golden cup resting on a ledge in the other cave, just near enough to be touched.

'I can see them! It is a book and a golden cup!' said Scheherazade. 'Stand up on my shoulder – look.' She could now see Tonto's face in the light. 'See – the light comes from there.'

'Well, that is the cup,' said Tonto, peering through. 'But who put it back like that? I drank from it, I knocked it over ... Someone put it back.'

Scheherazade stood up and ran her fingers over the stone facade.

'What are you doing?" said Tonto.

'Looking for a way through, of course. This wall is in shape like a door ... but there is no handle.'

Scheherazade stooped down again. She put her hand into the opening. Her fingers glanced over the cup. 'Tonto, what would happen to me if I drank from the cup?'

'If you should drink from it, I suppose your tongue would be loosened and you might speak a story that stops the world in its tracks – except you and I are stuck in a cave with no way out. I will happily listen to you tell a story. You have been good enough to listen to mine.'

Scheherazade stretched forward and found that her fingers could just grasp the stem of the cup, and she could perhaps lift it. But the cup was too large to pass through the opening. Whatever was held in the cup would spill completely.

She bent her wrist back and was able to snake a little finger over the rim and she felt liquid there. 'There *is* something in it ...'

She drew her hand back and licked the tip of her finger. 'It tastes bitter,' she said. 'It is like an unripe fruit.'

The taste spread into the back of her mouth, reminding her of aniseed. She felt tingling in her mouth. 'What do I do, Tonto? Do you think I could drink it one drop at a time? Is that enough? Or will it only work if I drink from the cup itself? And why does it taste bitter?'

'Perhaps the taste shows the kind of story that you will tell.'

Scheherazade looked through the opening. 'You mean that the stories I tell will be bitter if I do not drink rightly from the cup?'

'Sweet or bitter, we are stuck in a cave.'

'And I need to look into that book – for if I don't then, perhaps all I can tell is my own story, like you told me.'

'Well, it isn't a bad story, as stories go,' said Tonto.

The monkey looked over her shoulder. 'Papa said that in the book there are stories, pressed like flowers; but the cup gives to the one who drinks the power of telling. It gives such power that, when their voice is heard, the water that stands in a stone jar grows sweeter, and a fragrance like the scent of resinous trees falls from the wind.'

'*You* must have taken a big drink,' said Scheherazade with a laugh. 'Well, I will try to get the book. Dunyazad is already gifted with words, so perhaps all she needs is a new story.'

Scheherazade looked again at the book. It was not very large, and seemed to have hardly any leaves in it. She had expected something a thousand pages thick. But this smallish volume could pass easily through the opening, *if* she could reach it.

She reached in again. But she stretched too far. In a moment, the golden cup was dislodged and fell off the ledge with a clatter. She saw something like liquid gold splash out of it. The golden light was gone. In its place was a rumbling that shook the cave.

'Oh, Ersa,' said Scheherazade.

She drew back. The wall in front of them turned, pivoting on a central point (though it also felt as if the whole cave was turning round). Scheherazade clutched Tonto closely and slipped her hand through the opening, to grip the wall as it turned. They were dragged forward and around and when the slab of wall finally slid into place, they were on the other side, and fell forward into the Cave of the Five Golden Cups. Or that is what she first thought.

She crouched down until the rumbling had died away. When it was over, she knew that they were much safer than before, because now there was fresh air in front of them, blowing into the cave from the entrance some thirty paces away. She could see that outside this cave it was no longer night. There was a fog, and the shapes of trees. Before this, the only light had been from the book and the cup, which were now, she assumed, on the other side of the stone wall, back where she and Tonto had been trapped. She turned and looked again through the narrow opening. She bent down and scanned the darkness, hoping to see the book and the golden cup. There was no light, no shimmer of gold. The objects must have fallen to the floor. She reached in, felt around. Her fingers traced the ledge, but she could not feel the book.

She stood upright, angry, puzzled. She felt a flood of despair thinking that they had lost their chance and had been thrown out of the cave, empty-handed.

'It is cold,' she said, cradling Tonto, who had clung on to her the whole time. 'It was warmer back there in the other cave.'

'I think I prefer the cold and a way out into the open air,' he replied.

'Huddle close,' said Scheherazade. 'You are shivering.'

'*You* are shivering,' said Tonto.

She danced backwards and forward to keep warm. 'Will you go out of the cave?' said Tonto.

'Soon. There is mist, and rain. And the light out there is strange. I want to wait until it clears – see if there are soldiers out there. And the black thing that was in the sky. What of that? And is it always this cold in the Zagros Mountains?'

'I think we are not in the Zagros Mountains,' said Tonto.

'Let's wait a few more minutes. Please tell me the rest of your story.'

2

The Old Man and the Monkey

'I will take the quiet monkey,' said an old man.

The cabin boy turned and saw who had spoken. It was a man with a cap, whose hair stuck out sideways. It turned out that the man was a merchant of antiquaries. A lonely man who had run aground in that northern seaport. His family and the life he once lived had been snatched away. The little monkey could tell that look in the old man's eye.

The old man insisted that the cabin boy take at least half a gold piece. The boy sheathed his knife. The old man took the monkey and carried him to a warm room. The man fed him from his own plate in the inn where he stayed. He made sure that the monkey was well-wrapped and that he was let off his chain now and then, but only in the closed room. But the monkey did not run away, did not feel like venturing anywhere. The monkey was happier now, but he stayed as silent as when he had been snatched out of his forest home. The old man had a little embroidered jacket made and bought a beret that he gave the monkey to wear.

The old man one day took ship and sailed to a land in the south and made his way to a village in the forest that edges the Great River, in sight of Edessa. But this was not the forest that the little monkey desired. His home was a great distance away, and there was no-one to say, 'I will take this little monkey to its true home'. So the monkey stayed with the old man, neither sad nor happy.

One day, the old man was standing in a crowd outside the palace when the gates opened and there came out a parade of animals. First there was a giraffe, and then an elephant, a pair of leopards, and on the shoulder of a young man, sat a monkey.

The little monkey took a long time to see the truth, for the monkey wore no jacket or foolish cap on its head. It was only after the parade of animals had passed that he realised that the monkey was his very own sister. Perhaps, like him, stolen from his forest home.

After that, the little monkey went a little mad, and the old man thought it best to take the monkey on a journey, to taste the mountain breezes, and to hear the wild sound of the desert – these things were like health to the old man, but in truth the monkey cared little for these things.

One day on their travels they came to a magic cave, and there the little monkey tasted the drink from a golden cup and found he could speak. And then …'

'And then?' said Scheherazade. 'Don't stop.'

'The monkey became brave and with the help of Scheherazade came home to Edessa, and with all the strength he could find in his tiny limbs, he climbed the palace walls, and ran along the vast corridors, eluding the cruel guards, and finally found the place where they kept the animals imprisoned. And there he met the other monkey, his sister, and they wept for they had both been stolen from the same forest, from the same mother. And the other monkey, being wiser, knew the name of the river and the name of the forest and the name of the land from which they had been taken. And she knew his name and told it to him. He had forgotten his real name. Now he heard it again.

Then the little monkey hurried to find Scheherazade and spoke in her language the name of that land, the name of the river, the name of the forest. He said, 'Scheherazade, please take me and my sister home.' And because of their friendship, she said yes, and found a little boat and sailed with the monkeys to their home. And there, in a forest where butterflies dance in shafts of sunlight, where forest deer nibble the leaves, where the lizards do not have to wait long for an insect to fly by, and there ... there.'

3

Shay

Tonto seemed overcome with sleepiness – exhausted from the effort of talking.

'I will take you to the palace, when we get back,' said Scheherazade cradling him. 'We will find her. And we will go to the jungle.'

Tonto curled up in her arms and closed his eyes.

Light poured into the cave, as if dark clouds had rolled away.

To one side of the entrance to the cave was a pile of twisted logs and branches. The wood was wet from a curtain of water falling over the entrance of the cave into a bed of washed gravel. Scheherazade could hear through the waterfall a sound, like wind over rocks, and a loud low hissing.

She moved forward and stepped out of the cave. It was, as Tonto had said, not the Zagros Mountains. The door in the cave had been a magic door.

And someone was walking towards her. A figure was making its way with firm footsteps up a wet track beyond the cave. Scheherazade saw that it was a young woman, her own age, and that her hair was like the golden hair of some of the noble women of Edessa. She wore no veil, but did have a scarf tied around her head.

'Sister, there may be soldiers,' called Scheherazade.

The young woman turned and looked at her. 'She scanned the cliffs above. 'There's no-one else. Jus' the pair uv us.' She came closer. 'What's that in your arms? Is it a moggy?'

'It's a monkey.'

'It looks reet poorly.' The young woman unwrapped the shawl from her shoulders. 'Here, put this roond him,' she said walking up. She looked at Scheherazade. 'Can a touch you?'

The young woman touched Scheherazade on the arm. 'You're real. You're not a ghost. And you're broon like wor Hilda. And you've had a bit uv a crack on the head. Does it hurt?'

'It isn't bad,' said Scheherazade, feeling around her scalp.

'So, what are you doin' here?'

'I don't know.'

'Well, if you dinnah, a dinnah either.'

Scheherazade started to explain where she had come from.

'There's no time for any a that – am in a hurry. Let's get your monkey warmed up, though.'

Together, they wrapped Tonto in the shawl.

'You got workin' hands. Lookit mine. Not as bad as they could be, but maybe aal take t' housework soon, then they'll lose their hard skin and just look red raw from washin' and peelin' spuds. M' name's Shay, and what's yours?'

'My name is Scheherazade.'

'Shey-heruh-zayd? That's no good – the girls'll be callin' you Shey-for-short, and then you'll get mixed up with m'sel'. They'll be sayin', 'Hey, Shay' and we'll both answer and who knows where it'll aal end. I'd best introduce ee as Sadie, will that dee ya?'

Scheherazade was silent for a moment.

'And you're not one u the pit people, Sadie?'

'No.'

'Ah need t' keep movin'. You can waak wi' me 'f you like?'

'What is this place?'

'This? This place? These are the fells.'

'And what's that noise? In the air – a hissing, growling?'

'That's the Deep, doon thataway.' Shay pointed into the mist and down the hill. 'You cannit see it for now, but you will as we waak along.'

'What land am I in?'

'This? It's the land where you catch y' death, unless we leg it.'

'You have a home?'

'Aye, a've got a home … look, see through the mist? That's smoke as well. That's wor toon. Half uv it's burned. Come. You're pretty. A think we can use a pretty girl. Darren says am the prettiest in the toon, but a think he won't look at me now that you've turned up. Are y' strong?'

'Yes.'

'You've got muscle, aal gi' y' that. And a'll gi' y' a sack if you're willin' t' help.' Shay handed Scheherazade a hessian sack. 'We're goin' t' need t' gather a lot u jewels, and it's good you're here t' help me carry it then.'

'Jewels for?'

'For a weddin'. Haa'way.'

Shay walked on and soon they came to another cave. The caves filled the hillside.

'What is this place?'

'Ah've told y', it's the fells. It's a bit of a magical place, but reet now a haven't time for magic. How's y' little friend?'

'Sleeping, now that he is warm.'

Shay walked up to the largest of three caves and ducked in. Scheherazade nearly slipped on the blue-black stones, but followed.

'We're lucky,' said Shay in the gloom. 'A think we'll do well here. See in here – see these chests?' Scattered around the cave were some large wooden chests, dark wood with bands of black iron. 'They belonged t' the pirates, but they're aal gone in t' the shades.'

Shay picked up a rock and began to bang it on a rusted lock. Scheherazade looked around the cave and saw some metal rods. She took one, carefully laid down the sleeping monkey, jammed the rod behind the lock and with a thrust of her shoulders snapped the lock.

'That's the way!' said Shay. Scheherazade used the rod to prize open the lid of the chest.

'My,' said Shay, 'y strong as well as pretty. Now, haa'way, we've got t' gather all this in t' the sacks.'

Scheherazade looked inside the chest. Her mouth fell open when she saw the mounds of gold and amber and emerald jewellery – brooches, pendants, diamond crusted hair pins.

'And this is all sitting here in a cave on a hill?'

'No-one has much use for jewellery of this sort. It's a little bit ancient. But we have need owit now.'

'Why is that?'

'Am shy a tellin' ye. A hardly know what's happenin' m'sel, and a hardly know what am doin', and if a thought too much about it, then a'd be runnin' into the back a this cave and stayin' there till a was dead u hunger. It's as simple as this: The Beast King has takken ower the realm. He come in on a ship two days past. He sits on the throne in the castle now with the heads a wor aad king and queen stuck on pikes, and he demands a wife. The da's and ma's a the land are terrified, for the Beast King has summoned the daughters u the toon to appear this evenin' in the great hall, so that he can choose one and have his disastrous way with them. And a'm hopin' that aal be first in line.'

'What?' cried Scheherazade, backing away. 'This is a nightmare!' Scheherazade began to walk up and down, beating at the air. 'I'm inside the cave still and you are a dream!'

'Well, a was not expectin' that for an ansa,' said Shay.

'What is this place?' Scheherazade crouched on the ground near the entrance.

'It is the Land a Bernia the ancient kingdom on the east coast a the Great Islands, its chief business is coal and flint, tin, with some sheep and dairy ... I'd give y' another minute,' said Shay, 'if I had one t' spare. Obviously the little blue people of the hills have somethin' t' do with y' bein' here, but since ah've aalways been a daughter u the hills, and left out little offerins when I waak, then I'm not afraid for a start, and I do believe they've sent y' here t' help me. Sadie, listen, listen, now that y' here a have a plan. Sadie, do y' hear?'

Beads of moisture from the blowing mist were gathering on Scheherazade's face, and where she sat, water was dripping on her from the lip of the cave.

'The little blue people?' said Scheherazade.

'Have you spoken with em, then?' said Shay.

'I did,' said Scheherazade remembering. 'Oh, Ersa,' she said. 'I prayed in the temple of Ersa.'

'How's that?'

'The goddess of the morning mist has led me here. She is blue and small. I told her my troubles ...'

Scheherazade stood up and stared piercingly at Shay, but no more answer than her standing there was given.

'Reet, then,' said Shay. 'Will y' hold the sack open and we can get the trinkets stashed.'

Scheherazade and Shay filled two sacks with the spoils of one and then another chest. Scheherazade had to use all her strength to lever open the second.

'See! You're a gift,' said Shay. 'Aa'd never u prized this one open if y' weren't here. I daren't challenge you t' an arm wrestle, then, eh?'

Tonto still lay in the shawl that Shay had fashioned as a sling. Scheherazade took up the smaller sack of treasure with one arm, and with the other arm she cushioned Tonto, who looked to be snug and resting.

Shay twirled her sack onto her shoulder and the two young women set off. They took a path that brought them closer to the animal sound that rolled over everything. Through the mist Scheherazade finally saw the sea. She stood staring at it.

'Haaway,' said Shay, 'let's be havin' you – we can't stand open-mouthed aal day.'

The sea came up to the path they walked, which was along a low cliff top. A wave cracked open on a rock and a spur of foam jumped and fell lazily onto the rocks.

'See? It's just a geet lot a saltwatter. Let's get a move on, but not so as t' make us all red-faced and spoil wor looks.'

4

The Bridesmaids

The houses in Shay's town were built from a grim flint-coloured stone. The wetness of the day made the stone walls and slate rooves seem blacker than they might have been. All the houses were joined in lines, so that they seemed to Scheherazade like camels herded in a close line against a storm in the desert. The streets were cobbled, like a dried crocodile skin. Smoke hung in a pall, but a good deal of the smoke came from the many chimneys. She could see though that some houses had been blackened by fire. A horse lay dead on the street.

At the first house, Shay put her head in at the door and called out, 'Mr Chance, sir, is your Hilda in?'

A grim-faced man came to the door. His skin was dark as Scheherazade's.

'Aye, wor Hilda's home,' said the man. He spoke to Scheherazade. 'Don't see many like you oop this way, lass.' He turned back to Shay. 'You're not after goin' t' castle then? 'Tis certain death.'

Shay whispered in Chance's ear. His expression did not change, but his eye flicked towards the sacks, and over Scheherazade. 'Say that t' wor Hilda. If she agrees, then it's in for a penny, init?'

'Who's your friend, Shay?' said Hilda, pushing past. Hilda went up to Scheherazade and took her hands. 'Are you a cousin u mine then? Move out the way, Da.'

Chance pulled back into the doorway.

'Hilda, this is Sadie, from the hills. She's a canny lass – or leastways an uncanny one. Have you been cryin' then?'

'Givvover – it's just the smoke from the burnin' makkin' me eyes red. Have y' come up with a plan then, Shay Fletcher?'

'I have.'

'Let's have it then.'

Shay whispered in Hilda's ear. Hilda's eyes conned the sacks, flicked across Scheherazade, and said, 'Tis better than some uv y' mad schemes.'

'Go and tell the others doon The Row. I'll speak t' the eligible young lasses in Chert Street. Tell them t' bring their finery. Tell them t' think a dressin' as for the May dance at the Hoppin'.'

'You mean white smocks? That's not attractive.'

'Aye, it's too virginal. Maybe tell 'em t' dress for Summer Frolic. I suppose a little bit u ankle and shoulder will help things on. And get them t' brush their hair and throw on some perfume if they 'ave it.'

'Joanie has a big bottle a scent that the smugglers brought in.'

'Get her t' bring that and she can share it out t' those that don't have any.'

'If nothin', the smell'll stun the monster.'

'We can hope,' said Shay. 'Come, Sadie, let's get t' Chert Street. Hilda! Will you let go uv her hands!'

'I'll take care u you,' said Hilda to Scheherazade. 'You've got to watch out for Shay.'

The houses in Chert Street were pressed together as in The Row. Shay called in at various doors, but somehow the news had got ahead of them and a crowd of young women fell into step behind. Scheherazade saw that all the women wore much the same in black boots, ankle length skirts, white shirts and jackets with little variation in the pattern. In her sari and wrap, and wearing a veil and sandals, she stood out like a flower in a hedge.

'Are we goin' directly t' the castle?' called out one.

'No, Kathleen, we'll go t' the Mechanicals Hall and change our things there.'

There were now twenty-five young women walking. Fifteen more came from another street that fed onto the town square. They carried bundles of dresses, though one or two wore thin Summer clothing. These young women clutched their arms against the cold.

'It's perishin'! Who ud be mad enough t' have their troth night in the middle u Autumn?'

'I haven't had time t' put flowers in me hair,' said one.

'Then we'll pour on a cup u Joanie's perfume and no-one will notice.'

'It makes me eyes water just t' think on it.'

But there was little laughter and the group moved, on the whole, quietly.

'Well, Sadie,' said Shay, 'the Beast King will have plenty t' choose from. Though there's none as pretty as we two.'

Before Scheherazade could answer, a voice cut across. 'I won't have it! Shay – you must leave it t' us.'

'Darren Isaacs!' said Shay. A young man sprang from the doorway of a burnt house. The windows to the street looked like fireplaces, with tongues of soot up the walls.

'It's me young man,' said Shay to Scheherazade. 'Darren, get back in, before the soldiers see you.'

Darren came across. He limped and was accompanied by another young man with his arm bandaged.

'All u yuz, go back t' y' homes,' said Darren.

'And why is that, Darren Isaacs?'

'*We* will fight.'

'We? But the Beast King has cut half ower men down. He occupies the castle – you know that.'

'Who is this?' said Darren.

'She's none u your business. It's Hilda's distant cousin.'

'I don't believe that,' said Darren.

'Well no-one was askin' you t' anyway. Now shurrup and listen or you'll spoil everythin' …'

Shay pulled Darren by the sleeve close to her and whispered. Darren's eyes looked aside at the sacks and at Scheherazade. Scheherazade heard her say finally to Darren, 'So, gather everyone you can and rush in once things get bloody.'

Darren stood with his mouth pursed as if he'd found a small piece of gravel in his porridge.

'You'll never get a kiss with a face like that, Darren,' said Shay. 'Come here – it may be the last.' The two kissed. Scheherazade averted her eyes. Darren and his companion hurried away.

The Community Hall was on the far side of the square. The sides of the square were lined with small groups of people who looked at the mob of women as they walked into the Hall. As they went up the small set of steps out the front, a horn sounded from the ramparts.

Scheherazade looked up. The mist, always thick, had cleared enough for her to see the outlines of a large building with towers. She could see burning torches along a high wall that was dizzy to look at.

'It's the summons,' said one. 'We'd best be swift. I heard that if it sounds a third time and he hasn't got what he wants, then a prisoner'll be dropped from the walls every five minutes.'

Shay called over to a young girl. 'Ginny, get ower here. Sadie, this is Hilda's little sister, Ginny. Let her nurse the little monkey. She will take good care – she keeps a rabbit and a guinea pig. I need you t' stand with me, and you'll need both hands and you'll need t' be ready.'

Scheherazade handed the warm, sleepy bundle to Ginny, who went and sat on a bench.

'Will it wake?' she asked.

'I cannot say,' said Scheherazade. And she was worried that Tonto had fallen into an exhausted sleep after telling her the close of his story.

'What will it eat? Does it like nuts?'

'Yes. And fruit,' said Scheherazade.

'A can go find it some blackberries.'

Scheherazade heard a clattering. Shay had opened one of the sacks and dropped the contents onto the wooden floor. 'Here it is,' she announced. 'Treasure from the fells. Put on yer pretty dresses, pull off yer headscarves – y'll find earrin's t' clip on, brooches and ... Now a haven't introduced Sadie t' you all yet. A believe she's been sent by the little blue people. She was waitin' for me in the fells. We wouldn't have all these gee-gaws if it weren't for her. She is strong – not as strong as me – but she is the most beautiful one uv us here. And a hope that makes you all a little bit jealous. But a'll tell ee more in a minute ... Now get y' headscarves off and gan and get dressed. If we hear that horn again, we must walk up there, pretty or not.' Shay turned to Scheherazade. 'Sadie, here, can a have a quiet word?'

Shay took her arm and they walked to a corner. From there Scheherazade saw the other young women dressing, putting on the jewellery, combing out their hair. 'Ah've told them what a'm plannin',' said Shay. 'They all know what's t' happen. But you don't ... I think the Beast King will choose you. And when that happens a few uv us will waak forward as if we're y' handmaidens, lookin' pleased as punch. After that ...

well, a think it best that you don't know. But a'm askin' y' t' trust me. If you weren't here, then a'd be the one he chooses – well, at least a should hope so; but a also need t' be *not* that person, because a'm the strongest u this lot. That's where you come in. You will give us moments when he is distracted. You will need t' look happy when he chooses you. And if he takes y' hands, don't let em go for any reason. Look enraptured, and try not t' be sick.'

'Is he monstrous?' said Scheherazade.

'He's the Beast King.'

'Do you want me to put my hair up too?'

'Like the rest? No. Leave the hair doon,' said Shay. 'But put on some jewellery so that you blend in an aal wi' the rest uv us.'

Scheherazade found a bracelet and necklace, undid the clasp on the bracelet and put it round her wrist, and fastened the necklace on. She wondered if these pieces were from a tomb. She felt a shadow of death as the horn sounded for the second time.

'Let us go oop t' castle,' said Shay in a strong voice. 'Haaway.'

5

The Beast King Takes a Bride

The sound of boots tramping on the cobbles grew louder as the group of young women walked into a narrow cutting that led up to a courtyard. Scheherazade looked at the pretty dresses, the hair held in place by fantastically jewelled combs, and realised that the young women still wore their hard work boots. The dresses though concealed them.

As they came in at the gate, from which hung a contraption of metal spikes, a band of guards carrying torches and weapons ordered them to walk in single file with their hands in the air and the group came through the courtyard into the first chamber of the castle. Before they knew it they were in the Great Hall. Candles of yellow wax burned along ledges. A pile of books, scrolls, banners and clothing were piled high in a corner.

The young women stayed in a tight packed knot, as though they were sheep hemmed in by dogs.

'We will do well from the leftovers,' snarled a voice and laughter croaked around the stone walls.

Scheherazade felt the eyes of the guards especially on her. 'Oh, what have we here?'

A man in a brown leather tunic stood on a dais with his back to them. He was looking at something on a table – a rolled out map.

That's the Beast King, thought Scheherazade. From behind, he looks like any man.

'Let's spread ourselves out a little,' said Shay. She took Scheherazade by the hand and walked to the front of the pack. 'And one thing a didn't mention,' she said quietly to the young women. 'Keep yer eyes downcast. A know most uv y' can't help yersels, but try and look a little demure, if y' can. Except for you, Sadie – look him in the eye. Win 'im. For the sake uv all uv us.'

'Silence!' came a voice.

The man on the dais turned towards them. His face was all sneer. Two short horns extended from his forehead. Scheherazade dropped her gaze quickly. She kept her eyes low as a matter of habit, even though she knew there would come a day when she would look a man in the eye. The man wore highly polished boots ('Look up,' whispered Shay). Scheherazade saw from the edge of her eye, as the man walked towards them, that he wiped wine and grease from his lips with a cloth. He threw the cloth on the floor. Spurred by anger at his manner, she raised her eyes.

She watched him as he surveyed the group. Then his eyes lit on her.

'You,' he said softly. His voice was gentle.

He walked towards her. The Beast King was close now and looking at her with beautiful eyes.

'What is your name?'

She was silent, overcome, because the eyes were soft.

'Don't worry about your friends,' said the man.

'My name is Scheherazade,' she replied.

'*My Lord*,' said the Beast King.

'Scheherazade, my Lord.'

'You are not from this land?'

'I am a distant cousin of one of the women here, my Lord,' she said.

The Beast King looked around and sighted Hilda. 'Hm,' he said.

Scheherazade looked quickly at Shay, who kept her eyes fixed demurely on the floor. It seemed like a different person standing next to her. Scheherazade felt isolated.

The Beast King gave Shay a brief glance and returned his attention to Scheherazade.

'You are like a fruit of a strange tree, Scheherazade,' said the Beast King. 'Nothing like the fruit that grows in the stunted bushes of this land.'

She saw that he continued to observe Shay with growing interest, trying to gauge her reaction to his pointed words. Scheherazade did not need to turn her head to know that Shay was looking at the king with burning resentment. The Beast King returned his eyes to her.

'But what kind of fruit are you, "Scheherazade" – bitter, or sweet?'

Scheherazade saw his glance hurry back to Shay.

' – Wild, or poisonous?'

Scheherazade turned to see Shay looking at the king – her eyes were bright. Scheherazade could feel the edges of the plan being lifted as if with a knife. The other women were starting to fall into a tight knot, and soon there would be only Shay and Scheherazade by themselves.

'What kind of fruit, my Lord?' said Scheherazade. She raised her chin, bent her shoulder back. 'I am the apricot, known as the precocious one. That shines in a sweet brightness of golden velvet. That makes heavy the green branch. It is the saffron moon, injured easily by untimely frost or strong wind. My Lord.'

The Beast King looked away from Shay and went closer to Scheherazade, lifting a hand to touch her hair. His mouth broke into a smile. He had small tusks. But having spent time with Tonto, who had small, sharp teeth, and a sad voice she wasn't shocked. The Beast King saw this.

Shay's moment had come. The Beast King edged closer to Scheherazade. He looked down, with a slight raise of an eyebrow, and reached for Scheherazade's hand and twined his fingers in hers. She took a deep breath. The feeling of them was exquisite. Supple, cool, manicured. Everything she had imagined. For a long moment nothing existed except for the softness and coolness of his hand. And she thought briefly of Ishaq, who had abandoned her without a farewell, of Dunyazad who had happily gone to the palace to flirt with the king.

Shay's moment had come even more certainly. 'Me Lord, me hair's more beautiful than hers is. See! Have a look.'

Shay reached up and pulled out the brooch that kept her hair up. It was a jewelled brooch from the hoard of the ancient ones, with a sharp end.

'Why not choose me!'

The other young women responded as well. 'Don't even look at her! Me hair is more beautiful than that! Don't make me laugh – her?!' And they pulled combs from their hair and their hair shook out in a tumbling of red, blonde and brown. 'See, a'm as pretty as this one, me Lord,' cried one, stepping forward. The guards laughed. But the Beast King simply smiled and locked eyes with Scheherazade and smiled.

The Beast King worked her fingers. Their hands together were like one heart beating. Returning to the moment, Scheherazade reached forward and took his other hand. He firmly held her hand. Her heart was pounding and she thought, 'See how he looks into my eyes. I will need no story to win him.'

'I will be yours forever,' she said – these were the words of the marriage vow, and they had flown unbidden from her mouth. It was horrible, but she couldn't stop herself.

'I think you will make me … less of a monster,' said the Beast King with a sad smile.

Then Shay and the others, as one, leapt forward. With the spikes of their brooches, in a matter of seconds, they stabbed the king over a hundred times. The Beast King jerked back and tried to pull away, but Scheherazade held his fingers tight in hers, even though he tried to shake his hands free. Both her arms were nearly wrenched out of their sockets. She was screaming with the rest of them. She twisted backwards and pulled him off his feet.

Scheherazade found herself on the ground in a surge of boots, legs, crushed silk, floral prints and bony elbows. There was shouting and yelling and gasping and crying. She tried to stand, but her sandals slipped on the wet floor. Soon, the sound of fighting and swords clattering was coming from outside in the courtyard.

Someone was gently levering Scheherazade's fingers away from the dead grip of the king. Two of the young women were holding her. 'Get her off ground,' said Hilda.

Scheherazade had no strength to move.

'You can let go, Sadie,' said Hilda. 'It's finished, hinny. Let 'im go. It's done. It's done.'

Scheherazade didn't want to let go, but she did, and let herself be carried clear.

6

The Lamp

Scheherazade strode along the cliff edge with Tonto clinging to her shoulders. She felt as if she had drunk everything in the golden cup. She tried to stand still for a moment, but her legs kept moving. She couldn't stop them. She couldn't help herself.

The sun had shone as they all poured out of the Great Hall into the courtyard, laughing, singing, shouting. She wanted to be part of it, but something was forcing her to walk away. And she didn't resist. She wanted to be away from Shay as she wept over her young man, Darren Isaacs, killed in a final skirmish. She wanted to be back in her own world. She wanted the hills to hide her. She wanted to be rid of the frock and cardigan she was now dressed in. She didn't know whose they were; but she could not have worn her own clothes, not after the killing. Her sandals had to be abandoned – one had been torn off and lay soaked in blood – she now wore some boots and short woollen socks.

And yet she hated that her legs were not hers.

The town was gone. The path was rising, and before her lay the fells. She was almost running now, long strides.

Tonto sat on her shoulder and seemed his old quiet self. He now looked like any animal keeping secrets. Ginny had made up a little bag of berries and nuts, and he clutched this in one of his hands while holding on with the other. But he did not speak. His quietness frightened her. The paper bag of berries and nuts scratched against her ear.

'Are you going to eat those or not?' she said snappily.

He did not answer.

'Sadie,' a voice called.

It was Hilda, hurrying close to her.

'Sadie, you weren't off wi never a goodbye?'

'I ... I can't stop from moving, Hilda. I can't stand still.'

Hilda fell into step with her.

'Will you not come back and stay awhile? At least stop and have a meal.'

Scheherazade shook her head. 'I must go.'

'A know it wasn't pretty, I'll give you that. It was dreadful. A'd run away too. But there's those that didn't say it who want t' say thanks. It was a victory – and not just a little one. And we couldn' a done it if y' hadn' been there. But he's dead and it's done. Finished.'

'It's not finished,' said Scheherazade. She could still feel the touch of his fingers twined in hers. She held her hands in front of her.

'Why is that?' said Hilda.

'We do not touch lightly in my world. We do not take a man by the hand unless ... we mean to not let go.'

Hilda took Scheherazade's hands and pressed them in hers. 'There's no shame in what you did. Shay said t' me that you stepped out uv a different world. You were brought here by the little people. And t' you we're a dream. But a lot u things happen in dreams, that happen in the dream so that you don't have it gallivanting aboot in the light uv day. Do you hear what am saying?'

'This is more than a dream,' said Scheherazade. 'All that's happened here is waiting for me back in my world. This is my fate in my world.'

'Shay said as much. I asked her why you ran off and she said it's because you'd seen what has to happen.'

'Did she send you after me?'

'No. I said we should have you back here. She said t' let you go your own way. A thought that was a bit thankless, so a came out here u me own accord … well, let me thank you m'sel', Sadie.'

'My name is not Sadie, it's Scheherazade.'

'Shay … what?'

'Shay called me Sadie because …'

'It's easier t' say?'

'She said our names might get mixed up.'

Hilda looked at her with growing recognition. 'So, you are her dream, and she is yours?'

'I think that is right.'

'You're goin' back in t' the cave, then?'

'Yes. And back to my world. Or maybe not. I've seen magic, Hilda, and I hate it.'

'And what is happenin' in your world that you have to gan' back?'

'In my world a young woman has to be married to the king of our land, who has turned into a monster.'

'You have your own Beast King, then?'

'And each morning he has his wife beheaded and takes another in the evening. But if she spins a tale that pleases him, she will be spared. Might be spared. I looked in a magic cave for some stories that would win over the king, which I could give to my younger sister, because she has been put on a list of young women who must marry the king.'

'Why, that's awful.'

'It is only days away. So far I have found no story. Nothing. If I have found out anything from this dream, then it is I that must hurry back and take the hand of the king.'

'And do you then have the girls of your toon ready t' stand wi' you, and deal the blow?'

'No. I think not. To think of it, they are dead!'

Hilda replied after a moment, 'That'll be hard then. It's up to you, then.'

'Better let me go,' said Scheherazade. 'I will go ahead.'

'Must you go? You could stay here,' said Hilda, still walking alongside, with her arm in Scheherazade's and just keeping up. 'The girls think you're smashin. And I think you're more than just a little bit lovely.'

Scheherazade stared at the fells and the wind-torn trees. 'I would stay,' she said. 'It's wild, and it's beautiful … But …'

'Then do you want me t' come? You could use a helpin' hand perhaps? And in your world they all look more like me, don't they?'

'In my world, Shay would look unusual. You only see the paleness in the king and his court – they came from Northern lands. There is so *much* of it here, though! You must feel a bit alone.'

'I'm a bit of a rarity,' said Hilda.

But even as Hilda spoke, the blue sky vanished in mist and the sound of the sea fell away. And the tingling, driving noise filled Scheherazade's ears again.

'I can hear music,' said Scheherazade.

'It *is* music,' said Hilda. 'I can hear it.' She looked towards the caves, 'It's a summonin'. It's what's makin' you t' leap and run. Well, a suppose you must go, then. And a have to stay. If a went wi you, then there'd be a ghost u me wanderin' aroond here. Same for you if you stayed. Your people would see you, askin' them for help t' get back t' your world, bangin' on winders and the like to be let in. So, you must leave. And heaven help the one who tries t' stop you, an' that's sad.'

As she spoke, grey cloud swept down on them, shooting droplets of light rain.

'Come,' said Hilda. 'I'll waak wi' you, as far as a can.'

The cliffs now loomed over them in blurred, tufted shapes. Little beads of moisture lay on the wool of her cardigan. They came up the path and the entrance to the cave was largely the same as she had seen it that morning, the wet logs and the ribbon waterfall near the entrance; except that a small blue figure was now sitting on a flat stone and playing a fiddle.

As she and Hilda came up, the figure stood, seemed annoyed that they had taken their time, pointedly stopped its playing, and ran off as quickly as a dragonfly darts. The music was gone, but the notes still burned.

'Oh, you don't see that every day,' said Hilda. 'Only from the corner u your eye. Oh, what a grace that was.' She unpinned the necklace that she had worn to the tryst with the Beast King and walked over to the flat stone. She put the necklace on it, while at the same time keeping her eyes and face averted from what she was doing. She made a little curtsey and came back to Scheherazade. 'I'll have somethin' t' brag t' Shay about now.' Her face was sad. She whispered, 'I'd have come wi' y' – but the ones atop the cave say otherwise. It's just you.'

Scheherazade looked up. On the ridge of the cave above her stood two of the little blue people, carrying spears. The spears were only a foot long, but they were pointed towards Hilda. Hilda busily brought out from her shoulder bag a lamp – like a little turret-castle of metal and glass. She unscrewed the base of it, pulled out a box of matches, struck one and lit the lamp.

'Here, the lamp'll last a few hours. Shay said you were off t' caves, so I brought it. You keep it. Me Da won't miss it. If he does a'll say the little people had a need uv it. It's a light for doon the pit. I hate that you have t' leave. Is it far that you go in?'

'No, just a little way in.'

'Well, keep the lamp anyway. You can bring it out in after times and remember me by it.' She leaned over and kissed Scheherazade. 'Well, goodbye. I'd better go, or I'll be in trouble. Will you ever come back?'

'I'll try.'

'That'd be grand.'

Scheherazade turned and looked into the cave. Some small figures had appeared, not blue, but dark brown, so that all that could be seen in the shadows were their eyes gleaming and the outline of pointed ears. One carried the golden cup, another, the book. They looked directly at Scheherazade and withdrew into the deep of the cave.

Scheherazade looked back to see Hilda walking away down the path. Hilda gave a shy wave, turned away and was gone. Scheherazade walked into the cave, with Tonto quiet on her shoulder. The lamp gave out a pale light.

Scheherazade expected to see the little people again, but they had gone. The back wall was the same, with the slot opening as before. But, as she approached, she could see a glow of golden light spilling through from the other side. Bending down and peering through the opening she saw the book and the golden cup as she had first seen them. She gripped the ledge with one hand, grasping the lamp tightly as she did so.

'Hold onto me,' she said to Tonto, and she was happy that he seemed to understand and gripped tightly. With her free hand she reached in and knocked over the golden cup. There was a rumbling, and the wall seemed to spin round, though this time it felt as if the cave beyond had pounced on her.

part 5

The Battle

*

ᢁ There was once a young lad named Jabril who heard
that if you catch a leaf while it is still falling, then you
will have good fortune that day. He began to walk
around staring up at trees. And if a leaf began to fall, he
would chase it with all his might. But catching a falling
leaf is not as simple as you might think, especially on a
windy morning. You think you have it, but rest assured it
will spin past your fingers and land on the ground and lie
there laughing at you. Jabril began to walk into trees and
trip over roots, such was his desire to catch leaves of
good fortune. He was in despair of catching a single leaf
when he reasoned that he should wait until the season of
leaf-fall, when the red and bronze, yellow and gold
leaves fall in abundance. Surely he would have great
fortune then. He could even bundle all the leaves he
caught into a sack, and have a store of good fortune to
last him the year. Perhaps he could sell some of the good
fortune. But try as he might, when the autumn came,
even with the leaves falling like dead sparrows from the
sky, he caught nothing ...

from The Nights of Abu Nuwas

1

The Fate of Prince Achmed

Tarquin was now conducting most of his business in the Silver Room. He had, had the room remodelled since the execution of the queen. The solitary window had been expanded to give a wider view of the river, though fresh iron bars filled in the vista. Masons had been set to cut further protected openings. From the room he could now see what was coming in all directions. He had a bed brought in and slept there in preference to the royal suite.

The amber necklace had revealed everything.

Tarquin had written all of the visions from the necklace out onto scraps of parchment. They were spread across the central table, every dreamlike sequence, every curious fragment, and he moved them around to form meaningful patterns.

An attack by a lone assassin on a flying carpet was now a certainty, and vigilance was the key. Sentries with crossbows were hidden in the guard-posts along the walls. The guards had been drilled and instructed till they were beyond boredom.

Tarquin knew the exact night of the attack.

And he knew the identity of the assassin, though this was kept secret so that the guards would not underestimate the danger.

It turned out that Scheherazade, daughter of Jafar –
sister of the precocious girl in the apricot tree – was the
one who rode the carpet in his visons of the future. It
had taken him a while to realise that the figure was not a
small-framed man, but a young woman. The mystery
had been solved after it was reported that she had
disappeared, eluding the watchers in the forest. Tarquin
was forced to spend hours with the necklace and his
patience was rewarded. He saw Scheherazade travelling
across the desert for a secret meeting with none other
than Prince Achmed, son of the Sultan of the Indies.
Tarquin was horrified and angered that even his most
harmless-seeming allies were part of a vast conspiracy. It
was around that time that he realised that the carpet-
riding assassin of earlier visons – the assassin descending
past the apricot tree – was in fact this young woman.

He sent soldiers to apprehend Prince Achmed, who
was now imprisoned in the palace. But who were the
other conspirators? Were the merchants on that mule
train involved? How was it that Scheherazade worked for
King Zayn Al-Asnam? How did he communicate with
her? Was the old bookshop man her handler? There
were many mysteries yet to be solved, but soldiers had
been dispatched to find her in the foothills of the Zagros
Mountains.

Tarquin had long suspected a conspiracy, and his
suspicions had all been confirmed. He was, moreover,
inordinately proud of his strategy. Putting Jafar and the
girl Dunyazad in danger had caused Scheherazade to

break cover. The whole theatre of executing one young woman after another – inexorably getting closer and closer to the sister – had caused Scheherazade to disappear to join her fellow plotters.

And she did not know, or else hid it very cleverly, that her every move was foreseen by the amber necklace.

Tarquin realised that he now only had to sit and wait – and so, with nothing more to predict or plan, the loss of Amytis began to burn inside him. Knowing the night on which Scheherazade would launch her attack gave him time to kill. He spent it drinking wine to dull the pain and seeing off the next young woman who tried to tell him a story. Soon it would be the sister's turn.

2

Strange Meetings

The wall shook itself to a halt, the rumbling stopped. Tonto, with some help, took his hands away from Scheherazade's eyes. They were in the darkness of a large cave, but Hilda's lamp cast a clear light onto the floor.

Scheherazade touched the wall of the cave to make sure that it had stopped moving, then dropped down to look back through the slot. There were the cup and the book as they had been before. She could feel the moist air of the fells blowing gently on her cheeks. She stepped away.

'O Tonto, we are back in the first cave once again.' She cradled the monkey and looked into its eyes. 'Please talk. Why don't you talk anymore?'

'I'm scared that I'll run out of words before I see my sister.'

'Then drink some more from the golden cup!'

'No. I think I will have enough if I stay very quiet. And having told you my story, I feel a strong urge to be quiet. It's not that I can't speak; it's just that I'm too full to speak.'

'So, what do I do now?'

'Take me back to Edessa,' said Tonto. 'I will find my sister. What do you do? You go home, you take the hand of the king, and the monster will die.'

'Just like that?'

Tonto leaned over and put his hand upon hers and they sat in silence. She felt as if she sat on the edge of a calm sea that was hushed and waiting, and, like Tonto, did not wish to speak either.

After a few minutes some thoughts took shape. She had so far failed. She had not found a story, such as those which her father or Dunyazad told well; nor found the ability to speak it well. She had no charming words that Dunyazad could use to amuse. But it was clear that Tarquin did not seek amusement. So perhaps all that there was left to do was walk into the den of the savage lion, in place of all the other young women.

She thought briefly about reaching through to the golden cup once more, but decided that whatever magic was in the cup, it had a mind of its own, was wilful and dangerous. She might find herself thrown into a different world and be lost forever. It was well, she thought, that magic, on the whole, was locked up in secret places, high in mountains, hidden in caves, or in stories where you could close the pages on it and walk away.

She thanked Hilda in her heart for giving her the lamp – it hadn't occurred to her that she required a light to have any hope of finding a way to the surface again. In the lamplight she could see the contours of the passage they had come down.

'Come,' she said. 'We must leave here. What happened in that cave is the story that the golden cup gave to me.'

'And will your sister tell it to the king?'

'I will tell it.'

Tonto nodded and climbed onto her shoulder.

It was easier making her way now with a lamp. She saw the marks of her footsteps, and where she had crawled, saw the low hanging rocks, and did not need to stoop over. She came after ten minutes to the place where she and Tonto had slept after falling into the cavern. There were marks in the sand on the floor of the cave that showed that she had rolled down a slope.

Tonto ran forward, then came back a minute later. He gestured for her to come forward. She made her way up to one of the cavern walls and saw, a little higher than she could reach, a dark patch that must be the end of the chute they had fallen down. The lamp was only strong enough to outline the darkness of the chute.

Tonto climbed the wall easily and sat upon the edge of the opening.

'This is the way,' he said, sniffing the air.

Scheherazade found footholds in the cave wall and climbed up. Once at the level of the ledge she pulled herself in. She sat there for a few minutes, took a breath, crawled in, and forward, and made a point of not looking back.

The walls of the chute – perhaps a ventilation shaft, or a secret passage, or even a trap to throw prisoners down in days past – were sculpted, but not to marble-like smoothness. She could move along and climb upwards by keeping hands and feet pressed against the surface, or wedged against the angles of the stone. The heavy boots she wore had a good grip. Tonto climbed alongside, or else hurried on ahead, returning and nodding encouragement.

It was in a shallow section, though, that she slipped on some grit and slid back a short way. She pressed her whole weight against the stone, willed herself to be as heavy as stone, and stopped sliding. She recovered the distance carefully.

After long minutes, the chute came finally to a cave with daylight filtering in. The cave was choked with boulders. But through the gaps in the boulders she could see sky, and heard the sound of a thousand cicadas shrilling. She crawled along the ground between the rocks, for that was how she had got in during the night, and stood at last in the entrance of the cave where she had sheltered from the soldiers. She was back in the very place where she had hidden from the dreadful shape in the sky.

A man fell at her feet, as if he had popped out of the air, and lay there gasping on the stones.

She screamed and began to back away. Tonto retreated into the cave. The man lay there and began to speak.

It was Ishaq.

3

Return to the Shrine

Ishaq had nothing covering his head, and his face was burned by the sun. The shoulders of his black garments were caked in blood. With one hand he was holding onto a large piece of carpet that seemed to stand edgewise away from him.

She came towards him.

'Scheherazade, I knew it was you!' he cried. His mouth gave a smile that was quickly wiped away by a grimace of pain. 'Quick,' he said hoarsely, 'we must get away from here.'

He said some words and the carpet slid down beside him.

'It is magic!' she said. He nodded, rolled onto the carpet and fell back in a daze.

'Ishaq, Ishaq?' said Scheherazade. 'Is it *really* you? Dressed like this. What has happened? You are hurt! What is this carpet?'

His breathing was laboured. 'I knew it was you two nights ago hiding here ... but then I couldn't find you.'

'What?' shouted Scheherazade. 'Two nights ago? That is not right!'

'What are you wearing?' he managed. 'And ... here is Tonto ...' He stroked the monkey and fell back. 'I need water.'

His wish was the carpet's command. It began to slide away, with Ishaq on it, down the slope of the hill, and Scheherazade was left behind. She ran after it and called Ishaq's name. The carpet halted and floated on the air.

Scheherazade ran up and saw the confusion in Ishaq's face. She knew about carpets such as these from tales her father had told. Even after her journey into Shay's world, and the sight of the little blue people, and a king with tusks and beautiful eyes, she stood marvelling.

'You must ride with me,' said Ishaq, urgently. 'You must say a word before you are allowed to climb on,' said Ishaq. 'The word is *sirocco*, or you can use *breath*, or *spirit* ...'

Scheherazade said the word and the carpet closed the space between itself and the stony ground. Scheherazade knelt down on the carpet. She and Ishaq looked at each other.

'Is it really you?' he said.

There was just room for the two of them, and they sat close. And yet there still seemed to be plenty of space between them.

A drumming came to her ears.

Tonto leapt onto her shoulder and tugged her ear. He pointed.

From the far end of the valley seven men on horseback drove uphill towards them. More soldiers of King Tarquin and they carried bows and arrows.

Ishaq seemed to have fallen into a daze. The riders drew closer. One dismounted, notched an arrow as

Scheherazade stupidly watched him. An arrow sped by her head. 'Away from here,' she gasped. The carpet rose vertically into the sky. She reached over and held on to Ishaq to stop him from sliding off. The valley with its caves and riders fell away. More arrows coasted up towards them, but they failed to reach and dropped back to earth.

'Take us away from here,' she said. The carpet bore to one side.

She looked at the land sweeping along beneath her. The riders below shrank in size. She pressed more tightly against Ishaq. He opened his eyes and looked at her with curiosity. She was aware that this was a very public thing they were doing, but Tonto was with them, crouched between them, so she at least had a chaperone; but she also didn't care what people might say because her life was now so different now from when they had last spoken, and she wanted Ishaq there to wipe away the memory of the Beast King's touch. She took his arm and gripped it. But it was like holding on to a tree and she wanted to weep.

Ishaq began to speak, but his mouth and lips were dry. He looked pale. 'Water,' he said.

Scheherazade spoke to the carpet. 'The Shrine of Ersa. Please take us there.' The carpet changed course and curved away from the hills. It flew to the cliff edge – the village rushed past – and they were soaring above the path that lay beside the Fish Rock. They flew down the vast stone formation towards the desert. The carpet levelled out over the sand waste.

'Not close to the villages,' said Scheherazade. 'Fly so that no-one sees us.' The carpet edged itself further into the whiteness of the desert. They seemed to be sailing upon shimmering waves of heat. The hot air scorched them as they flew.

Scheherazade could see the villages clustered near the cliffs as burning silver shapes behind columns of heat haze. The carpet turned and she saw coming towards them the white bones of a dead tree, and the temple of Ersa, alone in the wasteland.

The carpet came to a halt by the little house behind the temple.

Scheherazade stepped down, called, and the old woman came out. She looked closely at the scene before her.

'O, my aunt,' said Scheherazade, 'I need water for this man.'

'You are the young girl who came here,' said the woman. She turned around and, shading her eyes, surveyed the desert and the cliffs. 'It is cooler inside the house. Bring him in. It is safe here.'

Scheherazade spoke to the carpet. It rose, moved into the house, and settled on the earth floor.

'You have been to the Zagros Mountains then,' said the woman. She went and found a water bag. 'Take this empty one to the well, my daughter.'

Scheherazade hurried out into the soundless intense day, quickly covered the hundred steps to the well, filled the water bag, and returned.

When she re-entered the house the woman said, 'He has fallen asleep, but it is not a restful sleep. His shoulder needs medicine. I will prepare a little food for when he wakes.'

Scheherazade excused herself and walked over to the shrine. She went in and knelt before the little blue statue, stretched herself out with her head upon the cool stone floor and wept.

'O goddess,' she said. 'I'm going to be too late, too late … Open to me today the river of your mercy, water me with full streams, from the springs of your grace, from the depths of your loving-kindness. I thank you that you have guided my feet through strange places inside the mountains and have brought me here again.'

There came a soft scraping sound.

'Speak,' said Ersa, a little out of breath. 'Tell me your troubles.'

'O goddess, I must leave very soon, and cross the desert tonight. I believe my sister was married today, if I have kept track of the days correctly – and have only this coming night to save her …'

'And will you take the young rebel with you when you leave?'

'I cannot take him,' said Scheherazade.

'Why is that? You can't leave him in the house.'

'Inside the mountains, where time turns upon itself, I saw that it is I who must offer myself to the king, and somehow vanquish him.'

'Perhaps you should not be telling me this ...'

'But if that happens, and I am victorious, then I have seen that my friend Ishaq will die in the fight, even though I live.'

'And how is it you know this?'

'In the mountain it felt as though I lived my story, ahead of its time; but I saw it as if in a broken mirror.'

'You have to be careful of things you see in the Zagros Mountains. They are not of heaven or earth. They follow their own rules. How do you know that what you saw is true?'

'I do not know. I do not know. Perhaps, o goddess, my story in this world will be different. For there will only be myself, not the many women whom I stood with when they rose up against their king.'

'You have had a time of it,' said Ersa.

'I will be alone,' said Scheherazade. 'I have no story to tell the king, except the one I have been through.'

'Maybe you need the young man – travelling by yourself across the desert is never a good idea. And you can't just leave him here for however long that takes. Does he know your plans?'

'No.'

'Does he wish to go with you?'

'We have not yet talked.'

'He is not well. Here is my advice. Take him first to the oasis of Al Borodin. There are healers there who can look at his shoulder. It is a nasty wound. From Al Borodin it is a few days journey to Edessa, but I think you will make good time. As to whether he is up to it, take the healers advice. But you should leave here very soon. The king's soldiers have been combing these paths. They came here to the shrine two days ago and searched everything. You must hasten. Though I think you should spend two minutes more here, in silence, by yourself.'

4

To Al-Borodin

In the house Ishaq lay asleep on the ground. His breathing seemed more measured, but it was still laboured, as if he was fighting sleep, or fighting the onset of fever. Scheherazade came from the shrine and found the old woman wrapping bread in a piece of cloth. Tonto sat up on a chair eating a date.

'Thankyou for your kindness. We have to leave,' said Scheherazade. 'We will go to Al Borodin.'

'I see the goddess has counselled you well,' replied the woman.

'I will wake Ishaq and we will go,' said Scheherazade.

'If you keep travelling west,' said the woman, 'you will come to a wadi. It swings back this way but it curves to the north. Double back along that – it will shelter you from watchers. When it gives out at the salt lake, go northeast. You will see the old paths to the oasis.'

Scheherazade bent over Ishaq and spoke to him. 'Ishaq, we must go. We are in danger.'

Ishaq opened his eyes and slowly righted himself.

'Why do you wear those clothes?' he asked.

'Why do you wear those?' she replied.

'Because I joined the rebellion.'

Ishaq, with proud eyes, told his story of how he was recruited, how he found secret passageways into the king's residence, how he had followed his commander

Gaspar to the Zagros Mountains, how he had lost all his friends, how the carpet they rode on had been torn in half to become two, then three, then many.

Scheherazade listened with her mouth open. Perhaps this was a tale to tell the king, except it would not amuse him.

'And then,' said Ishaq, 'the night that I saw you vanish into the caves I chased after you, but did not find you. When I came out, I saw that the men had lost control of the carpet. It rose high into the air and came apart. Men fell from the sky. I ran back to our encampment. But, as I came there, one of our commanders, Ali Zaybac, ran up to me in the dark, dragged me behind a rock and said I must not come back. He said that Al-Masudi had declared me a deserter, to be brought to him for execution. And my commander, Gaspar, had been killed by a *djinn* that Al-Masudi released on him.'

Here, Ishaq threw an arm over his face. A few moments later he looked up, his eyes etched with suspicion. 'Where is my satchel?'

'It is with your sword,' said Scheherazade.

Ishaq laid eyes upon it and became calm. 'Before I had time to find out more, there came a strange light around us. A *djinn* – in form like a man – came forward and laid hands upon Ali Zaybac and he was gone from my sight. I drew my sword and hastened to the encampment. I meant to kill Al-Masudi, to avenge Gaspar.

'As I came near I felt the earth tremble. Al-Masudi had repaired his "vessel" by again cutting pieces from the original carpet. I saw it ride up into the air with perhaps four or five warriors on board, and it vanished into the desert. I ran forward, but slipped and fell down a ravine. Branches and thorns tore at me.'

'It is a nasty gash you have,' said the old woman.

'I woke the next day having crawled into the empty camp and felt a shadow upon me. I thought at first it was Al-Masudi with a sword. But it was only the shadow of the carpet – this carpet here – floating on the air.

'As it floated it turned over once, then turned back again, like the palm of a hand turned down, then turned up. I don't know why it did this. But I understood from that gesture that all the carpets cut from this one were no more; that all who rode – and I think Al-Masudi with them – had perished over the desert. But Al-Masudi had other magic at his disposal, and perhaps he lives.

'I climbed on the carpet and went to have one last look at the cave into which you had vanished. You were fortunate to emerge when you did, because I have something I must do. You asked me, "Why am I dressed like this?" I am dressed like this because I plan to go to the palace, travelling on this carpet. I will go in by the secret way and kill the king. Now you must tell me what happened to *you*. Where have you been that you wear these clothes? And what is that thing like a lamp that hangs from your wrist?'

Scheherazade drew a breath, and was about to speak, when something made her sit back. The words were all there, or almost there, ready for her to say them. A feeling of calmness took hold of her – something she had felt sitting in the cave with Tonto. She felt that if she spoke, she could only say that thing once; and the story would not come out again afterwards if she had to repeat herself. She had to save up the words for later was how she felt. If it must come out, perhaps it was for the ears of the king. And he might, on hearing it, not kill her. And perhaps he would also not be killed. He might turn from being a monster. The softness of his hands and voice came back to her.

'I can't tell you,' she said.

'Why?'

'I cannot. All I can say is I have to go home, and you should not go.'

'What? Why?' said Ishaq. 'Why must it be secret what happened to you?'

'It is my story and I choose not to say.'

'I told you my story!' declared Ishaq. 'You asked me to tell you *my* story. It is not fair.'

'She only asked you why you were dressed this way,' remarked Tonto. 'You chose to speak.'

Ishaq and the old woman stared at the monkey.

'You are in no condition to fight,' said Tonto.

'I would scale the palace wall even if I were half-dead,' said Ishaq. He hung his head, drained. He lay back, gasping.

'You must go,' said the old woman. 'You, young man, are wounded, and your shoulder needs tending before you can think of doing anything.'

She opened the door. The sun was now golden and stood lower in the sky. The woman gave Scheherazade a waterbag, bread, and some figs, placed in a hessian sack tied with rope, and stood to one side. 'Oh, and take this blanket – you will need to keep warm for the desert air can be freezing. But I want it back.'

Scheherazade thanked her.

'I hope we will meet again,' said the woman. 'The goddess told me that she enjoys it when you visit.'

Scheherazade called to Tonto and sat down on the carpet next to Ishaq. The two rested close to each other, but there was now even more space between them.

'Al Borodin,' said Scheherazade. 'Through the wadi and the salt lake.'

The carpet rose into the air and sped away from the house, picking up speed until, with the wind surging over them, Scheherazade, Tonto and Ishaq had to lie flat. Tonto snuggled between the two of them.

Scheherazade had been given a scarf by the woman. Scheherazade was happy to again have a covering to protect her face from the wind and the dust. The dust made it impossible to talk.

*

Scheherazade woke to find the carpet gliding through palm trees. They were at Al Borodin.

Many people approached as the carpet came to rest on the sand and seeing Ishaq wounded they carried him into a tent. Scheherazade was invited to sit in a tent nearby where they brought her a plate of food. The healer at the oasis came to her and said, 'Come with me, my daughter.'

Scheherazade rose and followed to where Ishaq lay upon a low bed. Fabric soaked in water hung around him, and air from a wind tower sifted a cool breeze across him. The air was fragrant with healing herbs.

'The young man will recover,' said the healer. 'If he sleeps and if he takes his medicine. He desperately wants to rise from his bed, but wounded as he is, and lying in the open without food or water, this has drained the well. I believe also that he was recently poisoned, and is still recovering. The cloud is still in his eyes. I gave him something to clean the blood, to rest his mind, and to quell his ambition.'

'But he will live?'

'Yes. But only if he stays here to rest.'

Scheherazade stood still for a minute, looking at Ishaq, thinking she might say something, but decided it was best not to draw him back from the deep sleep into which he was drifting. She said to the healer, 'I must go. Say to him when he is awake, that I will return.' She quickly gathered up her things, called to Tonto and went outside. She looked at the carpet. The people standing around parted to make way for her. She said the word *sirocco* and sat down.

Tonto skipped away, then came back a few moments later dragging Ishaq's sword in the sand. He also carried a bottle of black glass.

'What is that?'

'It is from his satchel. Do you remember? In this bottle is a powerful *djinn*,' said Tonto. 'You will need it, for you will not have a band of women to help you.'

Scheherazade hung the sword around her neck and lifted the bottle up. The light of evening made it hard to see inside, and the flames from a nearby fire flickered along the surface.

'What do I do with this?'

'Break it open and make a wish when the time comes.'

She put the bottle into the hessian sack that she looped over her shoulder for safety. She embraced Tonto and said to the carpet, 'To Edessa.'

The carpet kicked up sand and cleared the palm trees of the oasis. Soon she and Tonto were sailing through the golden darkness of the evening. The heat of the day poured up from the shadows. But eventually the air cooled. She wrapped the blanket around her. After a while the moon, now at its full, came up. Tonto stared, remembering the moon upon the sea, but Scheherazade slept upon the carpet as it glided home.

5

The Peacock Courtyard

Hours passed. The moon was at the full and it was past midnight when she woke. Scheherazade sat up and looked down and saw the marshlands and forest floating by. The sound of drums, flutes and horns drifted up from beneath the trees. Bonfires and lamps gave away a village or a town. There were larger fires on hills. Rockets sparked up into the sky here and there.

'Tonto,' said Scheherazade. 'Listen! Tonight is the Night of Nights. It is when the windows of heaven are opened and the gods listen to the wishes of your heart.'

'Well, that is bad,' he said. 'People will be looking up at the sky. Someone will see us, and shoot arrows at us.'

Scheherazade asked the carpet to fly over the darker parts of the land, and they moved away from the course of the Great River, shining in the full moon. Several leagues further upstream she could see the rising wedge of darkness that was the walls of the New Palace.

'Take me to my house,' she said urgently. The carpet flew across the river and up the western bank. The tips of the trees rose towards her. Beneath her she saw the fire burning in Paribanou's courtyard. She saw people gathered there. In a moment the carpet slid past the apricot trees and Scheherazade was standing in her yard.

There were no lights in the house. Tonto jumped off the carpet to stand beside her. Together they walked slowly across the yard. At the door of the house Scheherazade lifted the latch and her heart fell into a dark well, for if anyone had been home, the door would be barred from the inside.

She pushed the door open and walked in.

'Father?' she called. 'Dunyazad. Are you here? D?' There was no answer. Her throat hurt. She could hear drumming and music from far off on the night air, but the house was still and dead. She called again. 'Father ….' She went straight to her bedroom. Her bed and Dunyazad's were undisturbed. In the darkness she ran her hand over the blankets. 'D,' she whispered. She remembered how once Dunyazad would hide under her bed when there was a storm. Scheherazade wanted to reach down and put her hand under that bed and be reassured there was someone sleeping there, feel her sister's back. But she didn't. There was too much danger of there being something else under the bed.

Time had broken apart while she was in the mountain, but she knew that her sister's marriage would be on the Night of Nights. She said to Tonto, 'She might, even now, be sitting on a cushion trying to amuse the king. The night is not over.'

She ran outside hot with anger, sick with regret, and climbed on to the carpet. It spun into the air and floated in circles over the house. She stared up into the night. 'To the palace,' she said. The carpet turned and flew upriver.

'Higher,' she said, seeing the tips of the trees only an arms breadth away. The moon was too bright, though now a night mist was covering the moon and making it a softer blue. She let the carpet float up, up, until the music of the villages, the bells and the drums and flutes, drifted away beneath her and the only sound was the low song of the moving breeze. Then she wailed and sobbed.

The crying helped. She wiped her face and said, 'Go to the Palace ... go higher still. Take me to the Peacock Courtyard.'

The carpet rose further into the moonlit sky, until Scheherazade felt that, even if they could be seen, she was so far in the air that she would be nothing but a speck in a corner of the sky, and that the dark underside of the carpet would shield her.

The carpet crossed the river and drew near to the palace. They drifted closer, then they were past the outer wall and the Tall Gates that faced the river. They were so high it was hard to see the moment when they crossed over the wall. Directly beneath them were the square shapes of buildings. The carpet began a vertical descent, sinking past the level of the upper walls, lined with guards looking out into the night, watching the fires, watching the odd firework that whizzed skywards, looking to the horizon for floating shapes.

The guards were unlucky, for a large bonfire near the palace, flaring up, drew their eyes.

'Keep going,' said Scheherazade, her face pressed to the fibres of the carpet.

The carpet was now gliding close to the rooves, like a leaf on a slow stream. A guard – too close – stood silhouetted against the sky. His spear flicked a moonbeam of blue light their way. Scheherazade could see his beard, but the man's gaze was outwards to the river, and the carpet was soundless. They were within the bounds of the main palace buildings, which now rose up to surround them, rising up on all sides until they framed a square of sky above them. The carpet settled. Scheherazade stepped off onto soft lawn. She was in the Peacock Courtyard. A small deer jumped away and looked back at her with shining eyes.

Scheherazade let her own eyes find detail in the shadows and she walked up to one of the walls. Her fingers touched the stone. She began to move her hands along the walls, searching for the door out of the garden that led up to the royal chambers. In one corner her hand struck a metal rung – part of a permanent ladder set in the wall and hidden among vines, which went to the top of the courtyard. She kept searching.

'Tonto?' she whispered. He was still sitting on the carpet, listening and sniffing the air. He ran over to her. 'She is here.'

Scheherazade crouched down. 'You mean, your sister?'

Tonto nodded. 'Yes.'

'Go and find her.'

Tonto looked thoughtful. 'Soon. Keep searching for the way in. I will help.'

'Oh, Tonto,' she said, pressing her face to his. 'I don't want to be alone.'

'We have come this far,' he said.

The secret entrance was not, in the end, hard to find. The way down from the king's bedroom was simply the way into the private courtyard and the door was clearly marked. There was a latch, not a lock. It was not an 'escape passage' as Ishaq had suggested, for it was a dead-end garden, apart from the worker's ladder.

But the courtyard was protected, for guards could walk at any time along the top walls and descend the ladder if needed. And now two guards appeared on their patrol. Scheherazade heard first the shuffle of feet (they walked with covered shoes so as not to disturb anyone sleeping) and a silhouette of their heads rose above the parapet of the courtyard wall. Scheherazade skipped back to the carpet. 'Turn over,' she said.

The carpet rolled, and the dark side showed itself to the sky. The lawn was in shadow and Scheherazade slipped under and hoped that, looking down, the guards would see nothing.

The shuffle and swish of feet moved along above her. There was a clink of metal against mail, followed by silence.

Scheherazade let out her breath.

There came a quiet chuckle. 'I hear you,' said the guard.

'What animals are in here tonight do you think?' said the second guard.

'Too hard to see in this light.'

'I thought I saw the gazelle. There! There is the gazelle – do you see her … tch, tch, tch.'

Scheherazade looked across and saw the legs of the gazelle. She held her breath and drew tight to make sure that her feet and arms were well-tucked in.

An object landed on the lawn and the gazelle started. It began to nibble at the object, a half-eaten apple.

'This is the best part of our watch,' said the second voice with a sigh. 'Better than standing guard outside the Silver Room, waiting for the king to suddenly appear,' said the first voice in low tones.

'Look there,' said the second voice. 'Someone has left a blanket on the lawn.'

'Or something has fallen in?' said the first guard.

'Shall I go down?'

'What? All you want to do is to sit in the garden and take your rest. I know you.'

'The ladder is here. It will only be a moment.'

'Alright – I'll hold your crossbow,' said the first guard.

Tonto squeaked. He skittered across the lawn and climbed the bushes that lined the yard. Clinging to a vine he put himself in view of the guards.

'Oho,' said the second guard. 'They've put you back in here have they? Nothing for you tonight. If I give you more nuts you'll be too big for that branch. Someone's been fattening you up.'

Tonto made squeaking noises.

'Not so loud,' said the first. 'Don't stir it up. We should go. We'll get in trouble for certain, the noise you're making. Small wonder he had the peacocks removed.'

'Here, have this,' whispered the second guard.

A nut fell onto the lawn near Scheherazade and Tonto skipped down and claimed it.

The sound of the two guards walking the wall diminished. Scheherazade climbed out from the shade of the carpet.

She hurried back to the door and lifted the latch. The door opened on well-oiled hinges. A spiral stair ran clockwise upwards, but the way was unlit. Scheherazade took out Hilda's lamp, but the tiny flame had long burned out and there was no time to try to find a way to light it. She put the lamp to one side in a garden bed, along with the waterbag.

She began to ascend the stair with Tonto following.

6

To the Red Room

The spiral stair was a thing she had never seen before, and it was not easy to climb. She reasoned that there would be no traps in it, and no-one hiding half-way. She hoped. The steps were wide at the outer edge and barely a toehold at the centre. Because of the absence of light, her foot slipped on the thinnest part of the step and she fell into the wall. She had the hessian sack over her shoulder and the contents clattered, but it was the sword she was carrying that made the biggest noise. The sword scraped on the stones with a sound that to Scheherazade's ears was loud and distressing enough to be heard through the palace. She could do nothing but stand still and wait, with her ears straining to listen for any responding noise. Tonto had curled into a ball with his hands over his ears. 'Don't do that again,' he said with a grimace. 'My face feels like it wants to drop off.'

'I don't need this,' said Scheherazade. She propped Ishaq's sword against the wall. She whispered to Tonto, 'Can you run ahead and see what you find?'

'Yes, and don't drop the sword again.'

'I didn't drop the sword.'

Tonto vanished upwards and came back a few moments later.

'There is nothing ahead but a door. The way is clear.'

Scheherazade kept on her way up through the screw of steps until she came to a landing and a closed door. This door was also held closed by a latch. She held the latch delicately and lifted it. The door swung forward, and she stepped into the king's bedchamber.

Directly in front of her was the reverse side of a tapestry. She moved sideways to be clear of it. There were small lamps, burning low, but enough light to see by.

She took a few paces forward. A tapestry rose up behind her with a pattern of a thousand eyes. A little moonlight came in some high windows, and closed doors led to a balcony. Furthest away, a bed stood against the far wall, surrounded by a structure like a pavilion.

A figure lay beneath the covers. Scheherazade ran to the bed. 'Dunyazad!' she hissed. But the bed was empty. What had seemed like a sleeping figure was only disturbed bedclothes.

'Your sister was here,' said Tonto, jumping onto the bed and sniffing.

There was a knock at the door and a man's voice, 'Dunyazad …'

Scheherazade backed away towards the window. 'Tonto,' she whispered, 'go down to the carpet. You know the words. Fly up to this balcony and wait for me.'

Tonto scooted away behind the tapestry.

The knock on the door came again.

On a stand at the end of the bed lay a folded robe. Scheherazade grabbed it and put it on over her foreign clothes. She left the hessian bag by the foot of the bed.

The door opened and a captain of the guard walked in with a drawn sword. 'I heard strange sounds.' His eyes ranged the dimly lit room, cautiously. Scheherazade moved towards the balcony window.

'Where are you going?' said the man in a plaintive voice.

'Where is the king?' she asked. 'Take me to him.' She had thought that putting on the robe might be a useful disguise. But she knew straightaway that the captain of the guard was not taken in.

Another man might have been tricked in the semi-darkness into thinking that she was Dunyazad. But not this man.

He levelled the sword at her. 'Who are you? And where is the king's consort?' he asked slowly.

She recognised his face and voice. It was Iram bin Ad, aide to Prince Achmed. He and Scheherazade had met in the desert.

'What is happening here?' he said in a low voice. He walked towards her. 'You were lost in the desert …

'I am Scheherazade.'

Iram lowered the sword. After a few moments he said, 'I thought your sister was in this room, waiting …'

'Waiting? For what?'

'Waiting for the dawn, of course,' he said. 'Waiting on the king's command.' His mouth was set and angry.

'She is alive?'

'For now. I assume … they must have taken her to the Pavement of Judgement, or perhaps to the Red Room.'

'You are Prince Achmed's aide.'

He shook his head. 'I was. The Prince was arrested after we came back to Edessa and found the land in turmoil. He is accused of plotting against the King Tarquin and is held in the Red Room, even at the risk of war with the Sultan of the Indies.'

'My father is held in the Red Room,' said Scheherazade.

'I know that,' said Iram. 'Your sister has told me. I could not help Prince Achmed. He was taken suddenly, his hands were bound. A noble foreigner …' She could see angry tears. 'You are her sister,' he said. He came close to her. 'She wept wondering where you were, why you were not with her, why you had fled, and abandoned her!'

'Stop!' said Scheherazade. 'I went to find her stories to tell the king. For when he takes a new wife he wants …'

'He does not want stories, or a replacement wife – he merely wishes for the leaders of the rebellion to show their hand. All this new-bride-every-night ploy is to simply pour hot oil in a serpent's nest. He has not been seeking a new wife; he seeks to find out those who wish to kill him. And you are the assassin, then! By the gods!'

'No. I don't wish to kill him.'

'But how did you get in here?'

'On a flying carpet.'

'Then it is all true. You are with the rebels!'

'No! I took the carpet … without permission. I came to save Dunyazad. I do not even want to see the king,' she ended mournfully.

'You will not see the king. He is drinking with his lords and closest confidantes, while his guards are on alert.'

'Help me find her,' said Scheherazade. 'I will take her away. Please. Take me to her.'

'The king lies in a stupor …' said Iram. Scheherazade could see thoughts flashing across his eyes. 'And you bear enough of a resemblance with the queen's robe on to be Dunyazad. You could pass for her … Strangely enough, the king's consort has rights. Come. Walk behind me. There is a guard outside this room, set by the king. Waiting for the assassin. When we step through the door, do not be surprised that they are there. But say nothing.'

Iram turned and walked out of the bedchamber. Scheherazade picked up the hessian sack and concealed it beneath the robe. She walked out following Iram onto a broad mezzanine. A squad of armed guards stood at attention.

'Hold your post here,' said Iram, 'We are going to the Red Room. There is no need for an escort.' And they walked past the guards and along a broad mezzanine.

The wall hangings, and carvings, and pointed arches, the moonlight pouring through high windows, were enough to make anyone gasp, but Scheherazade had been in magic caves and flown on a carpet, and it all looked rather small.

'What is it you carry in that sack?' asked Iram in a low voice. 'That thing you are hiding.'

'A powerful *djinn*. Trapped in a glass bottle.'

'I will trust to my sword,' said Iram. He turned to Scheherazade and said, 'Your sister and I love each other. She was brought to the palace after you disappeared. After Prince Ahmed was detained I was put back, demoted, to guard duty. I was set to guard your sister until her time came.'

'How is she?' said Scheherazade.

'Wretched,' said Iram. 'And you did not see her in the bedroom?'

Scheherazade had not seen Dunyazad, for her sister had fled the room when she heard the scraping of the sword, and unknown to Iram or Scheherazade, she was hiding out on the balcony, with the doors closed.

After descending two levels they walked through an arched opening into a large courtyard, the Pavement of Judgement. They were out in the moonlight, though lamps burning along the walls gave out most light. The Red Room was a wing of the palace with many underground floors, but the entrance was from the pavement, through set of black doors.

'Stop a little way behind me. Hold yourself with dignity. Let me go forward to speak.'

Iram walked up to the two guards who stood on each side of the door.

'Delivering the next one, sir?' said one of the guards.

'No, my friend,' said Iram, who turned to look at Scheherazade, realising that they had made a mistake. Dunyazad was not, after all, in the Red Room. He turned back to the guards.

'No. The king is indisposed, and the queen wishes to speak with Prince Achmed. I bid you, open the door at the king's command,' said Iram.

7

The Pavement of Judgement

As Iram spoke a man of senior rank in a blue coat came out from a side room.

'Who commands this?' he asked.

'The new queen,' said Iram. 'Who has rights when the king is absent. Let us not suffer anyone's displeasure by taking too long about our duty.'

The man bowed briefly and unlocked the door with a key that hung from his belt. The door mechanism rattled. The guards came forward, took hold of iron rings and hauled open the heavy doors. A wave of foul air poured out. No cave in the mountains had smelled like this.

Iram turned back to Scheherazade. 'I think she is not here, but I will free Prince Achmed …'

'Where is she?'

'We have been foolish …'

It was too late to think about anything else. There came a clatter of feet. Soldiers dashed out onto the Pavement from within the palace – almost as if they had been kept in hiding. The points of spears were levelled at Scheherazade and Iram. She had taken out the hessian bag, but a guard took it from her.

A voice barked, 'Drop that sword!'

Scheherazade looked to see Iram throw his sword down on the paving stones. She saw him looking at the hessian bag with its bottled *djinn*, now held by a soldier.

There was a sound of marching and calls to attention. Guards thronged the archway, but they split apart and Tarquin came out onto the Pavement, his face flushed. He looked at the open door. 'Close that!' he commanded. 'We're all very obedient tonight, aren't we?'

He looked at Scheherazade and Iram, his eyes flicking one to the other.

'Usually I hate being disturbed from the simple pleasures of being a king,' he said. 'But for this, I do not mind. For at last, it all falls into place, doesn't it? All the pieces of the puzzle. The secret rebellion. The plotters. The assassin, at last. And where is your flying carpet?'

'It is in the Peacock Courtyard,' said Scheherazade.

Tarquin turned on his soldiers and yelled, 'And has no-one discovered it?! No-one brought it here? You *watchers*? You attentive guards?' A flurry of guards disappeared back inside the palace.

Tarquin turned to Iram. 'All you had to do was accompany Prince Achmed on his holiday and report back any suspicious activity, or any sign that he was in league with Zayn Al-Asnam and the rebels. But, of course, you reported nothing, because you are in league with them. And this is how you repay everything I have done for the House of Ad.' He turned to the door-warden. 'Tell me, Captain, why was the door to the Red Room open?'

'Your highness,' came the shaky reply. 'Captain bin Ad requested it. He said that the queen wished to speak to Prince Achmed …'

'And does *she* look like the queen?' shouted Tarquin at the guards in a rage. He spun round, went close to Scheherazade and pointed at the robe she wore. 'Take that off. It is not yours. It will never be anyone else's. Take it off.'

For Scheherazade, everything was taking on a strange familiarity. She looked at the mass of guards, holding back a little, and she thought of the mass of young women who had suddenly turned on the king as soon as she had 'disarmed' him by taking his hands. Were these guards all here to help her? All the feelings that swept over her while Hilda tried to comfort her, returned. Something other than the death of the Beast King had been possible. Her heart had gone out to him. But it was too late in that world. He died. And yet here he was again. Not as ugly. Also not as beautiful.

'I think you will make me … less of a monster,' said the Beast King with a sad smile.

Her face must have shown something of her dilemma, for Tarquin slowed his advance. Seeing betrayal in every shadow, he also cast his eyes quickly over the guards, wondering what she was looking at.

Tarquin felt, like ice down the back of his jacket, that he was walking into a trap. He was sure that his guards were about to betray him, because had he *not* set many guards on the walls, and yet, here *she* was, in the heart of the palace? They must have let her in. And here was Iram bin Ad – *another* betrayal.

Scheherazade looked easily into Tarquin's eyes (she had already looked into the Beast King's eyes and felt at home there). In that moment she saw the pain as he looked at the garment she was wearing.

'What have I done to you, that you join with Zayn Al-Asnam and come here to kill me?' said Tarquin breathing quickly. 'And don't lie. I have seen you many times. I saw you sitting and plotting with Prince Achmed. I saw you travelling in secret through the desert. I've seen everything. Because I have an amber necklace – the treasure of kings – and in it I see images of what my enemies plan. I see that slug Zayn Al-Asnam laughing at me. I see the future.'

'It was you watching me all the time,' said Scheherazade.

'Yes. And I knew that you would be riding on a carpet, over the forest, this very night. To see me dead.'

'I came to save my sister. I came to offer myself to marry you if that would win her freedom. I crossed the desert only because I had to find a story, because I don't tell stories well … and I went to find that cave in the mountains from which all stories come, and it was a magical cave …'

'A magical cave, full of magical stories? And which story did you find?'

Scheherazade could not answer.

'Can't recall? Perhaps too busy learning how to ride a carpet? Well then, ours will be a short wedding night.'

'I found nothing. Instead, I was taken into a story.'

'What? Taken into a story? But what story? Tell me.'

'You must have seen it yourself, in the amber necklace.'

'No, I didn't. All I have seen is a woman in strange clothes coming on a carpet to kill me. In league with Zayn Al-Asnam.'

'I went into the foothills of the Zagros Mountains and there was a cave – one among thousands – and in that cave there was a golden book, and a golden cup that gives to the one who drinks the power of charmed speech ... but somehow I could not reach them. That is, the cup and the book. I tried, but I spilled the cup and then I found myself in a strange land in the mountains. It was like being in a story, but this story was like a mirror of this world. And it was real. There were people there. And in that world the king demanded to marry one of the young women of the city, and I was the one who took his hand ...'

She couldn't help looking into Tarquin's eyes.

'And what happened then?' he demanded. He suddenly held an open hand towards her. 'Here it is. Let's have yours and see what happens. Walk me through it. Sing it, if it helps.'

'Turn away from this,' said Scheherazade in a low voice.

'You fell into a story,' said Tarquin, coming closer, 'a story that was like a bead of amber – yes? – and you beheld the future?'

'Perhaps,' said Scheherazade. She felt like crying, but resisted.

'You met me in that story?' said Tarquin. 'That's it, isn't it? And, I ask you again, what happened then?'

'I saw ... that you were not a monster.'

He looked at her. 'I am,' said Tarquin in a voice she could hardly hear. 'Nothing more, nothing less.'

'I saw that you wanted not to be a beast, but ...'

She had taken off the queen's robe and now pressed it into Tarquin's hands. It twisted his heart.

'But what?' said Tarquin, throwing the robe to one side. 'But what? Here – take my hand – we will marry, and you can tell me the whole story. I'm sure I will be satisfied.'

Scheherazade backed away. The king held out his hand.

'Come! Squeamish? Take my hand. Or I will have your sister brought here and disposed of on this Pavement! And then you can have your turn!'

'No!' cried Scheherazade, and she reached forward and seized his hand. She clasped it tight and before they knew it, both their hands were clasped together. There was a leap of energy between them – they both felt it.

Then there was a crash.

Iram, on hearing that Dunyazad might be executed, there and then, in that moment strode forward and seized the hessian bag from the guard. He took the bottle out and threw it down onto the stone pavement. Pieces of black glass flew in all directions.

The *djinn* seemed to form from the available light in the courtyard. One of the paving stones cracked. And there was a massive face, like something in the back of a mirror, staring out hungrily. It looked at Iram and waited for his command. 'Your wish?'

But before Iram could speak, a guard fired a crossbow and it struck Iram in the chest and he fell backwards.

The *djinn* surged forward to stare closely in Iram's face. 'What – do – you – wish?' it said.

There was a loud crack.

Scheherazade found herself sitting upon the flying carpet. It was gliding down from the moonlit sky towards the Peacock Courtyard. Tonto was with her. The music of the surrounding villages drifted up. She saw the guards looking out towards the Great River. She saw the popping fireworks. She had the sword and the black bottle with the *djinn* inside. The *djinn* knew exactly what it had done, and that it had made a dreadful mistake.

Iram had not had time to command the *djinn* to strike down Tarquin – the crossbow took his breath away; but the *djinn* had read his eyes and understood Iram's last wish, his deepest hope, which was to go back and be outside the bedchamber with Dunyazad's kiss upon his lips.

The djinn had reversed time. But the *djinn* saw that it had brought about, not freedom for itself with a granted wish, but an endless loop of imprisonment. The bottle began to grow warm with its anger.

'What has happened?' squeaked Tonto.

'The *djinn* has brough us back to this moment.'

'I was by myself, on the carpet,' said Tonto, 'waiting by the balcony as you told me, but I saw Dunyazad! She was *on* the balcony hiding. We spoke. When she heard the scraping of the sword – ugh, that awful sound – she ran and hid on the balcony, thinking it was the king's executioners!'

Every moment since Scheherazade went up the spiral stair had now vanished like mist. But the memory of what happened was still in her mind. There was no time left to wonder why, for a bell inside the palace began to clang an alarm.

The two guards on their patrol leapt up a stair to the courtyard wall. One threw away the apple he was eating and whipped the crossbow from his back. A feathered shaft flew up and pierced the underside of the carpet. The carpet writhed and spat out the arrow.

'Away!' cried Scheherazade.

A trumpet now sounded the alarm.

High over the rooftops, out of bowshot, Scheherazade saw what she must do, and that she had only minutes to do it.

'To the Pavement of Judgement, to the door of the Red Room,' she said. 'As quick as we can.'

The carpet picked up speed and flew around a watchtower. More arrows flicked past them. The many guards set by Tarquin on the walls were doing their duty. A spear passed between Scheherazade and Tonto. The carpet angled away into the darkness and found a new way of approaching the Pavement.

'Tonto,' said Scheherazade, 'in the courtyard there is a man wearing a blue coat. He has a key to the black doors – it is the place they call the Red Room. We have to open the doors, and free the prisoners. Father is there.'

'Blue coat. Key. Red Room. Black doors. Prisoners,' said Tonto. 'Will there be more than the one man?'

'There are three, perhaps.'

The carpet dropped suddenly down to the stone pavement. The blue-coated man had been in a side room when she had previously arrived, but now he stood in the open courtyard, dazed, with the two guards and their captain standing uncertainly. They all had memories of the king talking, and the *djinn* appearing. From their point of view, since they had not moved very far in space in the previous minutes, everyone had simply vanished.

'Now!' said Scheherazade, leaping off the carpet. The blue-coated man turned and ran. Tonto skipped after him. 'Give me the keys!' he squeaked. The man screamed in shock. One guard leapt forward, but Tonto ran between his legs. Another of the guards with a swing of his spear sent Scheherazade stumbling backwards. She tripped and fell. The man had the spear at her throat in a moment.

'Do not move!'

Tonto ran back and jumped up on the guard and bit his ear. The man cried and tried to shake the monkey off his head.

'Why do you need the key?' demanded the soldier, who was protecting the man in the blue coat.

Scheherazade suddenly realised that she did not in fact need the key. She reached into the hessian sack, brought out the black bottle and smashed it on the ground as Iram had done.

Once again, the *djinn* erupted into the air and filled the courtyard with a roar. The guards were thrown back from its presence. A darkness sucked up the spare light.

Scheherazade slid over the floor as if pushed by a breaking wave.

'What is your wish?' said the *djinn*, with a disgruntled snarl. It pointed a yellow finger at her. 'And no tricks this time!'

'Throw open those locked doors,' cried Scheherazade. 'Please.'

'Is that it?' said the *djinn*. 'Imprisonment just for this? Isn't there a key for that kind of thing? You call on me to open a door? I who can divert the streams of time, untwist the strands of fate?!'

'Then throw the guards in the river as well!' said Tonto leaping up and down. 'And claim your freedom, O great and loquacious …'

Before he could finish speaking the black doors blew outwards and the *djinn* vanished. The guards were not to be seen, though boatmen at rest by the river heard a loud splash.

Scheherazade ran into the Red Room. Steps down led to a filthy open space crowded with captives.

8

Prince Achmed Again

'Is Prince Achmed here?' cried Scheherazade.

Prince Achmed was standing with a small crowd of dishevelled prisoners. They were hard to see in the meagre lamplight.

'I am Prince Achmed,' he said. 'Something very strange has been happening. The doors opened, the doors closed … You … we met in the desert. The king insists that we are conspirators.'

'Do you have the tent?' said Scheherazade.

'The tent?' said the Prince.

'You purchased it in the Zagros Mountains, it was a gift for your cousin …'

'Oh, dear,' said Achmed, his face filled with despair and laughter. 'The piece of cloth that I bought to humour that old trinket seller, the one that is supposed to hold an army!'

'Do you have it? Take it out!' said Scheherazade.

The Prince hesitated.

'I flew here on a magic carpet, found in the Zagros Mountains. Whatever you have, take it out. It is your last hope. Tarquin is coming here.'

Achmed looked at her. He reached into the right pocket of his coat. The pocket was empty. He shook his head, then reached into the left pocket and brought out a square of fabric wrapped in faded ribbon.

There came the sound of running beyond the doors. Someone shouted a command and arrows flew into the entranceway and studded the open doors. The captives who had begun to ascend the steps fled back down.

'Everyone stay back,' said Achmed. 'Here, let me open this.' He tore off the ribbon and unfolded the napkin, quickly but carefully, and suddenly there was more fabric than before. He put it on the floor and opened it up further. The fabric now seemed like sailcloth. The Prince called for help and the fabric grew with each unfolding.

'It is a tent,' said one. 'It *is* a tent!'

One more unfolding and ropes were now visible, and some poles, and tent pegs.

'Let me!' cried one prisoner. 'Tents are my trade.'

The tent was swiftly pulled upright and guy ropes stretched out and held firmly.

A voice called from the courtyard. 'The rebel Scheherazade will step out now.'

The Prince looked at Scheherazade. 'So, are you part of the rebellion?'

'No. I came to free my sister from death.'

The Prince raised empty hands to an unknown god. 'This whole ... conspiracy of his is a deranged fantasy. Save us from the madness of kings!'

'But,' said Scheherazade, 'there is a rebellion ... they are few and now scattered in the desert, or have perished.'

'May I speak on your behalf?' said the Prince.

Scheherazade nodded.

'You out there,' called the Prince, while men finished pulling on the guy ropes, 'are armed to the teeth, while the lady you seek is defenceless. Furthermore, she is no more a rebel than I am and we will not hand her over to injustice.'

'Send her out now, Achmed, or all of you down there die.' It was Tarquin. 'Do you hear me!? All of you! I knew you were plotting against me. It is proven!' If rage was Tarquin's protection against pain, he was making very good use of it.

'Friend,' said Achmed, 'nothing is proven. Send for the Judges of Samarkand and end this terror. Put your evidence before them, call for testimony. There is no-one in here who seeks your downfall.'

There was no answer, only silence.

'My friends,' said the Prince turning to the other captives, 'as you can see, this tent has certain magic qualities. I purchased it in the Zagros Mountains …'

'Then Heaven save us,' said one.

Another shower of arrows crashed down the stairs, followed a moment afterwards by twenty swordsmen, crying in loud voices.

'Open the tent,' said the Prince.

The canvas was flung back.

Nothing happened for a few seconds.

Then white horses with mounted soldiers – female ninja in glittering blue and black armour – poured out, with shields and long spears. The horses launched themselves up the stairway and the riders met the incoming swordsmen with a clash of steel. Either they pushed the swordsmen back into the courtyard or rode over them. More soldiers poured from the tent, some carrying smoking muskets and finally there were four small war-elephants.

On the Pavement in front of the doors lay the carpet, where Scheherazade had dismounted, and when someone stepped on it, they somersaulted to one side. Scheherazade came out in the rush of prisoners, with Tonto clinging to her shoulder. She saw a guard flung through the air and ran to claim the carpet. In an instant she and Tonto were rising into the air over the Pavement of Judgement. Through the archways that led back into the palace she saw the guards falling back, scattering. But a small knot of Tarquin's lords were fighting hard. Some fled up a broad staircase and were brought down with arrows. Muskets fired and smoke gusted through the corridors.

Scheherazade saw Tarquin fighting, but lost sight of him. Tonto squeaked, his little arm pointing. 'There, there!' She saw Tarquin leaping up a staircase, with a sword in his hands. He was running in the direction of his apartment and to the bedchamber, to where Dunyazad lay, she supposed, hidden on the balcony. Tarquin's lords closed up the gap behind him.

'Oh, quick,' she said. 'Out into the night!'

The carpet swept in a fast arc over the Pavement, up and around the outside of the palace. The carpet seemed to know what her wishes were, even before she spoke them. The moon swung overhead. Scheherazade felt her stomach rise into her throat as they swooped down a steep flight of air to the balcony. She heard a scream, and a shout of a man in a rage. The carpet stopped so quickly that the air was pressed from her lungs, but Scheherazade stepped from the carpet gasping and ran into the bedchamber.

'Sister!' she cried. 'Dunyazad!'

Dunyazad sat on the bed and looked at her. Iram stood nearby, his sword drawn. It was red with blood. He gripped his wounded arm.

The room was as she had first seen it, with the bed and the tapestry of a thousand eyes, the low lamplight. But now the eyes of the tapestry looked down upon a figure lying on the floor.

It was Tarquin, and he clutched his side.

'Well,' said Tarquin, through gritted teeth. 'You again. Have you another genie in a bottle somewhere? To rewind the world. Now is the time for it. Or else the wedding's off.'

Scheherazade looked away from him and ran to Dunyazad and they embraced.

'You came at last,' said Dunyazad through tears. 'I thought I was alone.'

'I was angry and it made me reckless,' said Scheherazade. 'I am sorry I left you.'

'But if you had not …' Dunyazad gripped Scheherazade's hand. 'Forgive me for anything I did which brought us to this,' she said. 'I flirted with him in the apricot tree, not for him, but because of you. To show that I was the clever one, and worthy …'

'But you are!' said Scheherazade. 'You are the storyteller, you make our father happy with the words you speak.'

'When did words save anyone?' said Dunyazad.

Iram, who stood between them and the king turned and said, 'You are safe. He will hurt no-one again.'

'The night is all twisted,' said Dunyazad. 'Someone whispered that an assassin on a flying carpet would enter the room, and I was the bait for the trap. Then I heard noises from inside the wall and fled to the balcony and who should there be but Tonto on a magic carpet, speaking to me.'

Tonto climbed into Dunyazad's arms and with his small hand stroked her face.

'You spoke to me, didn't you?'

'I did,' said Tonto. 'I am a storyteller, now. We can have a competition.'

There was a crashing sound of falling ceramics and a door smashed open. A war elephant stood in the doorway, and 'soldiers of the tent' stepped in.

'At ease,' commanded Iram. There was a silence.

'The king holds a weapon,' said a voice.

'It is no weapon,' said Iram, who had kept his eyes on Tarquin all this time.

Scheherazade looked to see Tarquin clutching a jewel. It was the amber necklace. He held it to his face and stared at the dull shapes. He let it fall, looked up at Scheherazade and began to speak, but the words were not loud. She walked over and looked down. His voice, always a little thin and raspy, was now a coarse whisper, so she moved closer.

'I feel this could have been different,' he said.

'As do I,' said Scheherazade.

'Can you ask Prince Achmed to do whatever is necessary to remedy the evil I have done,' he said. 'Express my shame to my father-in-law, the Sultan of Akkadia. If you will it, I would like a northern burial. Do you know what I mean by it?'

Scheherazade knew about a northern burial from tales that her father had told them – the king's body placed in a boat with sword and treasures and sent out upon the waves, sometimes on fire.

'We must say *farewell* to each other,' said Tarquin. 'Was this part of the story that you lived through?'

'No,' said Scheherazade.

'It is now,' replied the king.

A few moments later Iram walked over and declared, 'He is dead. Edessa has its honour once more,' said Iram to those in the room. 'Let everyone who can rejoice.'

'I do not feel glad,' said Scheherazade. 'I feel that somewhere there is a world where he and I lived together, but it is now lost.'

'Lived together? But at what cost?' said Iram.

Prince Achmed came into the room and he went and spoke with Iram. 'My friend. I heard that you were killed by a crossbow. But we live to greet another morning, and I am glad.'

Scheherazade told Achmed what Tarquin had said.

'I will send to Samarkand for a Judge,' said Achmed, 'as I said before. Someone who can decree justice, and order recompense. But I feel that Edessa will not last much longer in the tally of small empires. The Sultan of Akkadia will want more than words of regret for the death of his daughter. There may be nothing left to give. Scheherazade, you have freed those wrongly imprisoned. Do *you* wish for anything?'

Scheherazade summoned the flying carpet and said to Achmed, 'Can you place the king on this carpet?'

Achmed called for help and Iram and others lifted the body of the king onto the carpet.

'The northern kings are buried at sea,' said Scheherazade, 'with jewels and weapons and rich clothing.'

Scheherazade found the embroidered robe still folded over a chair. She could not believe that she had worn it barely minutes before, yet here it was folded up still. She took it and draped it over the king. In his hand he still held the amber necklace. Achmed placed Tarquin's sword by his side. The soldiers of the tent came forward and placed weapons around him.

'It is well done,' said Achmed quietly. 'There are many who would see him dragged instead through the street.'

Scheherazade went over to Dunyazad. 'Is there anything you want me to do, or say?' she said quietly.

'No. I meant nothing to him. He means nothing more to me.'

Scheherazade knelt and said to the carpet, 'Take him to the sea. Lay him safely there, then go to the place that you choose.'

She stepped back and the carpet rose and glided through the open windows of the room into the end of the night and was seen following the course of the Great River down to the sea.

9

The Night of Nights

'Scheherazade,' said a small voice. Scheherazade was standing again in the Peacock Courtyard looking for Hilda's lamp. Soldiers and courtiers had followed her down the spiral stair. Tonto was calling from a tree. It was darker now in the courtyard. Next to Tonto was another small monkey, whose hand he held.

'You found her,' said Scheherazade.

'It is my sister. Her name is Tchi-t'tchi. And she told me my name. It is Oud-wo'ud. I'm so happy! I had forgotten it. And now will you take us home to the jungles of Moxambique?'

'Moxambique?'

'That is our home. That is where our mother lives. You promised me that you would.'

'Of course I will,' said Scheherazade. She cried, because the end of Tonto's story was simply happy, and not troubled, as hers was.

'Do not cry. You have done well,' said the monkey. 'Very well. But I would have kept the carpet.'

'I wish the carpet would return,' said Scheherazade. 'What was I thinking? Because I would fly now to the Shrine of Ersa and give thanks. And I'd find Ajedro's grave and we could say our prayers there. And find Ishaq, and see that he is well. And fly to Moxambique and take you home. But now I must find a ship, or a mule. I hear they are better than a donkey for a long journey. Come with me up the stair?'

'No,' said Oud-wo'ud. 'We will stay in this garden until we leave.'

'I'll go and find some fruit.'

'No. Tell someone to bring it down! Ask one of these people. You have won the kingdom – everyone looks on you as the new queen. Give some orders. I would.'

Scheherazade returned up the spiral stair.

The first person she met on re-entering the building was Iram, who came and told her the news. Dunyazad had found their father in one of the lowest dungeons of the Red Room and had brought him out. He was weak, but alive.

'Take me to him, please,' said Scheherazade.

They found Jafar lying on a sofa in a side room off the Pavement of Judgement, holding Dunyazad's hand. He would have jumped up, but he could hardly move. Still, he embraced Scheherazade and they wept together and laughed, and Jafar comforted her, even though his arms were thin and he had lost a lot of weight.

'Everyone talks about you with awe and wonder,' he said. 'What have you been doing?'

Prince Achmed, who seemed keen to be near Scheherazade, asked if he might listen to her tale.

She told the whole story of her journey, how Maruf helped her elude Tarquin's watchers, and of the death of Ajedro, who, she imagined, died happily thinking of the Cave of Tales. Jafar wept to hear. She told how she and

Tonto had found, not a story, but something more strange, and fateful, that brought her to the king. She told Jafar how Tonto – or Oud-wo'ud – had found his sister.

'It needs a little polish,' said Jafar at the end. 'Perhaps fewer characters; but what a strange story.'

'It's a fine story,' said Dunyazad. 'How could it not be? Except I would change one or two things. When I told the tale of the Moon, the night before I came to the palace, it was you, Scheherazade, not I, when we were very small, who first asked if we could bring the Moon home. It was you who said to our father that perhaps we could put a blanket on the floor and make room. It was I who wanted to search for the amber Tears of the Moon to find out who my many suitors would be. Yours was always the deeper wish. And I would set the story straight here on this Night of Nights.'

'It is the Night of Nights?' said Jafar. 'I have lost track of the days. I do remember that night in the forest, with the Moon following us home. But, Dunyazad, I think you will need no more of amber ...'

Iram came forward and took Dunyazad's hand. They both knelt before Jafar. They asked for Jafar's blessing on them. He clasped both their hands in his.

'But someone will need to annul the marriage to Tarquin,' said Jafar.

'It is annulled with his death,' said Iram. 'Let us talk no more of him. With your permission, sir, I will take your daughter away from this place to the house of my sister. Will you join us there?'

'I would gladly, my son, but I cannot walk yet, and I don't wish to be carried. I want to walk out of here in the daytime.'

Scheherazade leaned over. 'Sleep now, father,' she said. 'It is almost the morning. I will stay here with you.'

'But how can I sleep?' said Jafar. 'I came out of the grave to find both my daughters alive in a world of wondrous things.'

The next day, Scheherazade returned to the forest, accompanied by attendants that Prince Achmed insisted should walk with her for honour. She went to the bakery and was greeted by Maruf and his sons. Al-Haddar was quite overcome and they had to find him a chair. Paribanou bade Scheherazade sit for breakfast and brought her a mint tea. Many people from Ajedro's village and the surrounding villages, hearing that she had returned, came to the courtyard to greet Scheherazade and thank her on behalf of all the young women who no longer had to face the cruelty of Tarquin. It was a day that later became known as the Day of Gratitude. Scheherazade returned to the palace that evening to be with her father.

10

Many Meetings

Prince Achmed made it his business to visit and talk
with Scheherazade every day and helped her navigate the
politics of what happened next. He sent messengers to
Tarquin's father, Montague, and persuaded him that it
was safe to return from exile and rule Edessa once more.
Montague agreed to come back.

Montague had been known in his day as the
Peacemaker; now he had little choice to do otherwise.
Edessa was now under threat from the Sultan of
Akkadia. His armies came to within a half-day of the
city. The campfires and siege towers could be seen from
the walls of the palace. But instead of defending the
realm, Montague walked out and surrendered the whole
of the Edessan kingdom. The region thus became a state
of Akkadia. The city was renamed Al'moheda, and
Montague became the Emir.

Judges from Samarkand came in those days and
decreed gifts of restitution for the families that had lost
daughters to Tarquin.

King Zayn Al-Asnam came with emissaries to
rebuild the bridges of friendship and spoke on behalf of
the nearby desolated kingdoms. He expressed mild
confusion when Prince Achmed over the banqueting
table asked about one of his commanders, Ibn Al-

Masudi. Al-Asnam said he could not recall having heard the name.

'A clever man, I believe – knows a lot about carpets,' said Achmed.

'Doesn't ring a bell,' replied the Al-Asnam.

It was assumed that Al-Masudi had perished when the many carpets became one single carpet again, and that he fell out of the sky onto the desert floor. But no-one actually witnessed his death.

When the Akkadian commanders entered the city and marched to the palace, Scheherazade, standing with King Montague's party, was surprised and pleased to see that Ishaq was with them. He had recovered his strength, and his clothing was no longer that of a rebel warrior, but a young commander. Afterwards, they spoke together. Ishaq told her how the Akkadian force had passed through Al-Borodin on its way north, and Ishaq had offered himself to the command as one with knowledge of the palace. At first, he only had thoughts of liberating his people, but had discovered that becoming a lieutenant in the Akkadian army unlocked something for him, and he wore his uniform well. As a soldier under a commander, he understood, he said, why Scheherazade had had to abandon him in the desert, without so much as a goodbye.

'It was not *abandoning*,' said Scheherazade. 'I discovered that I had to return to the palace and put myself in the way of the king. But in doing so, I saw that you would die in the fight. And I did not want that.'

'Well, I felt abandoned,' said Ishaq, 'you departed from the oasis swiftly, and you took my carpet …'

Scheherazade had to explain that the carpet seemed to be its own mistress, and having taken Tarquin away, it had not returned. She also said that *he* had first of all abandoned her, pretending to have gone off to seek his fortune, without the smallest goodbye. Ishaq said that he supposed that was true.

Later, Ishaq found a role as a delegate to the Sultan of the Indies on behalf of the Akkadians and rose in rank as a diplomat. There was though, very soon, a chance for Scheherazade to set Ishaq's mind at ease on one matter. She met Gaspar, Ishaq's friend in the resistance. It came about this way.

Scheherazade asked if Prince Achmed would help her restore Oud-wo'ud and Tchi-t'tchi to their home in the jungle. Prince Achmed said that he would gladly assist such a hero, and a ship was provisioned. Prince Achmed said that he had done as much as his position allowed to restore peace in Edessa and his absence would allow Montague to be more himself. He would, if she desired, travel with her on her mission.

The voyage set out from the Great River. Jafar was well enough now to travel with them. He was keen to spend as much time with an open sky above him as was possible. Three of the ninja princesses from the magical tent had decided to remain in this world, and they too came on the voyage.

The boat and one or two other barges travelled from a downstream port of the Great River into the estuary of Abodjan. At night, everyone sat up on the wide deck, telling stories and singing, and Jafar was in the mood once more to tell a few tales. Halting at an island one day, they found Gaspar son of Ahab. He had heard of boats coming south from Edessa and was keen to hear news of the turmoil. When he learned in advance that Scheherazade had flown into battle on a magic carpet, he sought to meet with her. They spoke together of their separate adventures and news was sent back up-river to Ishaq of Gaspar's survival.

Later, Gaspar went to live with Ishaq and his family after Ishaq married. Gaspar himself spent many years afterwards petitioning the Judges of Samarkand on behalf of the families of Al-Nadim, Jali'ad and Shimas. Eventually King Zayn Al-Asnam, to keep his involvement quiet, sent them gifts and settled the matter 'out of court'.

Scheherazade's ship continued on the journey to Moxambique. When they came to the Indian Sea, there were storms and adventures, but the party eventually found its way to the mouth of a river and, from the small town there, travelled upstream in smaller craft to where the jungle was hot, and where butterflies danced; where forest deer nibbled at the fruit cast off by the monkeys, and lizards and skinks batted away the insects because there were too many to bother eating.

It was a bright morning when the boats halted before a set of rapids. They could go no further upstream.

Tchi-t'tchi could hardly contain her excitement.

'Here, it is here!' said Oud-wo'ud. 'This is the place.' He and Tchi-t'tchi skipped off the narrow boat and disappeared into the green jungle.

'Come,' said Scheherazade, and she and Jafar followed, splashing into the stream.

'But where do we go?' said Jafar. 'What if there are tigers?'

Even though Tchi-t'tchi had gone ahead, Oud-wo'ud quickly reappeared and waited for Scheherazade.

'Go with me, please,' he said.

'Is this your home?' said Sheherazade.

'I believe it is,' said Oud-wo'ud, his little eyebrows heavy. He stood with his mouth pursed. 'I believe it is.'

'We have walked into more frightening places,' said Scheherazade.

'I don't know. Will you take my hand?'

'Of course,' said Scheherazade.

The two friends walked on together, stepping over old vines and matted undergrowth. Jafar, Achmed and the rest of the party followed a little way behind. Oud-wo'ud kept craning his head upwards to look into the high branches, but saw nothing. He climbed up on Scheherazade's shoulders for a better look, but he saw no monkeys running along the branches.

'They are not here,' he said. 'Where are they?'

Scheherazade tugged at his hand and Oud-wo'ud looked down, for they were now standing in a clearing. A family of monkeys was gathered on the forest floor, looking at them. Oud-wo'ud climbed off Scheherazade's shoulder. He could not speak. Tchi-t'tchi was holding the hand of an old monkey, who slowly came close to Oud-wo'ud and touched him gently on the face. She said some words and embraced her missing children.

*

Scheherazade and her party prepared to go downriver as evening came on, for Jafar was worried about tigers prowling at night. The sky was misty green. As they climbed into the boats, Oud-wo'ud came to Scheherazade and sat quietly in her lap. He had not spoken since meeting his family. After a long silence he climbed out onto an overhanging branch. The other monkeys were not with him.

'I will miss our little talks,' said Achmed. 'Farewell, my friend.'

'Goodbye, Tonto, friend of Ajedro, and protector of my children,' said Jafar, making it sound more like a funeral speech than he intended.

'Oh,' said Scheherazade, reaching up and taking his hand. 'This can't really be goodbye.' A few of her tears fell into the river.

Oud-wo'ud said, 'Eeek, t-cheek, eek ...' and stopped himself. He coughed, held up a hand, then said huskily,

'The magic *is* fading. For the story is told, and I have come home. I will become a quiet monkey again.'

'Not here,' said Scheherazade. 'You have your family now. You will have much to talk about.'

'We have done marvellous things together, you and I.'

'We have,' said Scheherazade.

The river tugged at the boats to pull them away.

'The jungle here is smaller than I remember,' said Oud-wo'ud. 'O, Scheherazade, in a year from now, send for me, and you and I, let us visit the caves once more.'

'Yes. Of course,' said Scheherazade.

'And find the cup again and take a really big drink and fix the world.'

'Yes. I will come back here. In a year,' said Scheherazade. 'I'm so glad you've said this. I couldn't bear to part here and for this to be the end.'

ᗄ There are many stories of Scheherazade. In one she marries Prince Achmed; in one she does not. In one she discovers that by rubbing a lamp she is able to bring her friend Hilda from another world, and they travel together and have many adventures. In one she and her faithful monkey solve the mystery of The Lost Plates of Atlantis. Another story says that Scheherazade married Tarquin and amused him for a thousand and one nights with breathtaking stories until she had, in this order, prevented her own execution, given him three children, and caused him to express some regret for his violent behaviour. He did not though make recompense for his cruelty to the daughters of Edessa, rather he was pleased that 'they could now all move on with their lives'. Some say that in every tyrant there is a diamond of soul that can be saved, given the right woman; others that kings are scoundrels who should reap what they sow. And yet others say that these are the kind of ridiculous stories you find in abundance in the Zagros Mountains.

from The Nights of Abu Nuwas

Acknowledgements

Many thanks to Petrina Barson, Helen Bell, Lucinda Gifford, Peter Haydon, and Ashley Sievwright for reading the early drafts. Thankyou Lucinda for the beautiful cover. Thankyou to Andrew Farrell of eBookAlchemy. Apologies to anyone from the northeast of England for the rendition of the Geordie accents; and apologies to anyone who lives in the Zagros Mountains. There was an actual short-lived County of Edessa, a 12th century Crusader state ruled by Baldwin the First and Joscelin the Last (*not* Montague or Tarquin). The idea of the carpet that multiplies, but returns to being the one carpet, was inspired by the sacred stone in Charles William's novel *Many Dimensions* (Gollancz, 1930). GT